MEG EASTON
Clean romances with fun-loving, unforgettable characters

The Christmas Pact

This is a work of fiction. Names, characters, businesses, places, events, and incidents are either the products of the authors imaginations or used in a fictitious manner. Any resemblance to actual persons, living or dead, or actual events is purely conincidental.

Cover Illustration: Alt19 Creative

Interior design: Mountain Heights Publishing

Author website: www.megeaston.com

THE CHRISTMAS PACT

MEG EASTON

MOUNTAIN HEIGHTS
PUBLISHING

The Christmas Pact

For everyone who has found a love of Christmas and to those who are working on it.

Contents

CHAPTER ONE

Noelle

Noelle Allred held her cell phone to her ear, veering to the other edge of the sidewalk as she walked under a mechanical lift that held a man in its basket, draping Christmas lights from one side of Main Street in her hometown of Mountain Springs, Colorado, to the other. She could hear her sister, Hope, on the other end of the line, telling her four-year-old son that he couldn't tie his two-year-old brother to the dog so he could ride him like a horse without falling off. And that they couldn't do it, even if the brother and the dog both acted like they wanted to.

Snow was softly falling from the morning sky, promising to make the lights extra beautiful when they turned them on for the first time tonight. It was something that Noelle used to love, but not anymore. She adjusted her hood so the flakes wouldn't land on her hair, melt, then dry weird on the way to work and make it look like she'd just woken up and hadn't even glanced in the mirror before heading to work.

She shivered and pulled her coat a little tighter.

"I'm back," Hope said, a little breathless. "I had to play the 'Santa's watching' card, and I'm not proud of it. But I also think we avoided a possible concussion in Porter's near future, so I'm working on being okay with it. Back to tonight—what time are you planning to be at Downtown Park for the tree lighting?"

Noelle adjusted the strap of her bag on her shoulder and braced herself for her sister's response. "I'm not going."

"What?! Why not? You've never skipped. Not even for those four years when you were in student housing. How can you not come tonight?"

She took a deep breath and glanced at the shops on Main Street, which all seemed to be trying to outdo each other with their Christmas decorations and window displays. Then she immediately dropped her eyes to the snow falling onto the sidewalk in front of her. "It just doesn't feel right to go with Gran-gran gone." The pain of her loss stabbed her in the heart again, like when the grief had been brand new. She stopped to lean against a building for a minute and just looked up at the snow falling.

Hope was quiet for a long moment, then whispered, "I miss her, too."

Noelle's family was big on Christmas. Actually, that was an understatement. If Christmas was a TV screen, it was the JumboTron at Ball Arena in Denver to her family. If it was a trickle of water spilling over rocks, it was her family's Niagra Falls. If it was a figurine for most families, it was the Statue of Liberty to hers.

And Gran-gran had been the leader of it all.

Noelle didn't say anything more, so Hope filled the silence. "I know it felt that way last year, but that was because she'd just barely passed away. I think it'll be different this year."

But Hope hadn't been as close to Gran-gran as Noelle had been. None of them had been as close. This year felt like it'd be worse in part because she hadn't just passed away. They weren't busy planning a funeral this year, going through all Gran-gran's things, and deciding what to do with them. This year would feel like a regular Christmas, but it'd be missing the most essential ingredient.

"I don't think it will," Noelle said, making herself keep walking toward the bus stop just in front of Downtown Park, a block further down the street. "So I'm just going to skip Christmas this year."

"Skip it? I don't understand."

"You know..." Noelle said, waving her hand around, trying to encapsulate everything, but realized the motion was pointing out all the decorations on Main Street. "I'm just going to pretend like Christmas doesn't exist."

"You can't just skip it."

"Yep, that's what I'm doing. I am officially done with Christmas. This is no longer the Christmas season; it's simply the winter season. Look—I've got snow all around me just to remind me that's all it is. I'm going to avert my eyes from anything remotely Christmassy." She cupped her hand beside her eye to block out the view.

"Excuse me!" someone called out. Noelle jumped and took a step back as four guys—who had been blocked from her view by the hood of her coat even before she had blocked them even more with her hand—crossed just in front of her, carrying a workshop table for Santa's village that was being set up in Downtown Park for the start of the Christmas festivities tonight.

So much for averting her eyes from all things Christmas.

"There's no way that you, the biggest Christmas lover of all, is done with it."

"No, I am."

She reached the bus stop, which gave her a view of the park that was even worse than her view had been walking down Main Street. A couple of people were working to install the false sides to the big gazebo to make it look like a giant gingerbread house. They would be serving hot cocoa inside during the festivities tonight and at a few other events during the month.

A life-size manger scene was set up on its right, complete with the stable, Mary, Joseph, baby Jesus, a donkey, a handful of sheep, and a shepherd.

To the left of the gazebo, several volunteers were working on getting Santa's village set up, which was a massive undertaking. The village had half a dozen elf houses, red and white-striped street signs, Santa's sleigh, several reindeer, stacks of wrapped presents, and a big outdoor workshop where a dozen elves worked to make toys.

A few more volunteers worked to set up the train tracks and the small working train that would carry the little kids in a circle around the entire workshop. Lighted arches led the way to where the train could be boarded.

And a couple people were stringing thousands of lights on the massive pine tree that stood in the middle of it all. There was so much activity and movement in the park that it kept involuntarily pulling her attention to it. Looking the other direction only meant that she'd be watching people wrap the street lamps on Main Street in garlands.

And not only that, but the bus was late—probably because of the snow. Noelle couldn't exactly keep her eyes closed and still watch out for the bus, so she caught loads of Christmas happenings. No amount of averting her eyes and using her hand as a blinder could keep it all out. And even though her hood was nice and fluffy, it didn't keep out the Christmas music playing for the workers setting everything up.

"Do you really think that you're going to be able to do that?" Hope asked. "While living in Mountain Springs and while being a member of our family?"

Hope was four and a half years older than Noelle, and she was married and had three kids. So they were at very different points in their lives, yet Hope was her best friend. Or, at least they had been as adults, even if they weren't even close to best friends as kids. Now, though, Hope was the person she could share anything with.

Noelle sighed and rubbed her forehead. "It might take a lot more work than I was anticipating. Why did I have to slide on that ice and make my car inoperable right now, of all times?"

She'd bought her car three years ago for her birthday after falling instantly in love. She was the cutest car, not too big, and was the perfect Christmas red. She'd named her Elfie right on the spot.

The only bus stop that would take her from Mountain Springs through the canyon to Golden was right in the middle of everything. And to get to it from her house, she had to walk right down Main Street, so there was no avoiding it all. If she had her car, she could take a wide drive around downtown. She could find a path between her home and work where she could bypass it all.

"I might be skipping all the Christmas festivities, but I'm still going to buy presents for everyone. So there's no way I can afford to fix Elfie anytime soon." People were important, even if Christmas wasn't for her anymore.

"So, what are you going to do?"

She shrugged and squinted through the snowflakes on her eyelashes and all the falling snow to see if the bus was close. "I've decided I need to get a side job so I can save up enough for the repairs. Lots of places are hiring temporary help at this time of year, right?"

"Yes," Hope said, dragging out the word. "Lots of places. Like places where people do their Christmas shopping."

"I hadn't thought of that." Noelle shivered and switched her phone to her other hand so she could put the one that had been holding it in her pocket. "What am I going to do? I can't just wait until after Christmas to get a second job. I don't want to wait that long to get it fixed, and that's when businesses are least likely to hire."

"I don't know, but I'll keep an ear out for you."

She perked up when the bus lumbered around the corner, heading her direction. "Thanks, sis. My bus is here, so I've got to go."

"We'll miss you tonight!"

"I'll miss you, too."

But she wouldn't miss the big reveal when they turned on all the lights and everyone ooh-ed and ahh-ed over the big tree and everything else they were setting up. Nope, not one bit. All of that excitement and anticipation for Christmas had left with Gran-gran. She turned her back on all of it—the decorations, the people setting it up, the Christmas music—and climbed into the bus.

She took a seat in the middle right as a Christmas song came on the radio. The six people seated in the back started singing along to it like they were carolers standing outside someone's house, bringing joy and all that. Noelle pulled her hood a little tighter around her ears and tried to pretend like it was just winter. That's all they were doing—singing winter songs.

She could do this. She could one hundred percent skip Christmas this year.

CHAPTER TWO

Jack

As Jack Meadows neared his sister Rachel's small house, he could see that the eight inches of snow that had fallen during the day covered her driveway and walks. Even though Mountain Springs was only a thirty-minute drive through the canyon from his home in Golden, it included a two thousand foot climb in elevation. He sometimes forgot how much more snow that meant that his sister got than he did. Snowplows had cleared the roads, thankfully, so he parked in a mostly clear spot in front of her house.

He responded to a few urgent work emails on his phone, then got out of the car, pulled on his hat and gloves, and opened his trunk. This time of year, he always kept good boots in his trunk for days like this. He traded his dress shoes for the boots, wishing he was wearing something other than suit pants, and tucked them into his boots. He would have to remember to leave a pair of jeans at his sister's for times like these.

Then he trudged through the snow and entered her garage door code. He grabbed the snow shovel, switched on the outdoor lights, including the Christmas lights, and then went to work shoveling the snow from the sidewalks and driveway and piling it on the already two-foot-high pile of snow in her grass.

His mind was on work as he shoveled, which wasn't different from any other time of day. He loved having his own ad agency, but it definitely took every bit of his focus while he was awake. And remembering the dreams he'd had last night, he had to admit that his laser focus didn't really sleep when he did.

Eventually, he finished, stomped off his boots, and traded them back for his dress shoes. Then he pulled his car into the driveway, just in case the snowplow needed to come by again while he was inside—the skies didn't look like they were quite done covering the world in white.

As he walked toward Rachel's front door, he marveled at the Christmas lights on her house and trees. A neighbor must've put them up. He and Rachel never once had Christmas lights growing up. He wondered if she had asked for help or if a neighbor had just felt extra Christmassy and wanted to spread it to others.

He used his key to unlock the front door. The moment he had it open, his five-year-old nephew Aiden shouted "Uncle Jack!" and raced toward him, launching himself into the air as he neared, clinging to him like a starfish. Jack gave the kid a tight hug. Their golden retriever, Bailey, had followed right behind him, giving a single bark before panting, wagging her tail.

"Hey, buddy! How are you doing?"

"Good," Aiden said as he slid back to standing on the floor. He grabbed Jack's hand and pulled him toward the open kitchen and family room. "Momma and I were hoping you'd come. She's extra sick today."

Oh, no. He should've left work early. When they got to the family room, he saw Rachel sitting in the recliner, looking pale and weak—worse than when he'd seen her yesterday. He immediately went to her side. He knew that this round of chemo was a tough one, but he hadn't expected her to look quite so sickly.

"Why didn't you call or text to let me know you weren't doing well? I would've gotten off work earlier and brought food."

She reached out for his hand, so he gave it a squeeze. "The—" Her voice came out like a squeak, so she cleared her throat. "The neighbors brought dinner over."

Aiden jumped onto the couch next to his mom in a sitting position, bouncing as he landed. "It was chicken soup and the best cornbread muffins ever."

"Oh yeah?" Jack asked.

Aiden nodded.

Jack looked at his sister. "Were you able to eat?"

She nodded. "Some. Today's just been a rough day."

"What do you think about moving into my apartment in Golden for the next little while? Then I could respond more quickly and help more." Maybe he should get her a live-in nurse.

"I don't know anyone in Golden," Rachel said, "and I've got a good support system here. Plus, I wouldn't want Aiden to not be able to go to school here—it's where all his friends are. My church here organized everyone to bring food for the next few weeks, and they come to check on me often. I feel well cared for."

He nodded. "Do you want me to move in here for the next little while?" It would definitely require some significant adjustments, but he was willing to do whatever would help.

"I do!" Aiden said.

But Rachel chuckled softly. "No. We really don't have the space. But do you mind helping me to my room? I'm just feeling a little weak right now."

Jack scooped her up and carried her into her room that was just off the family room. She felt lighter than the last time he'd had to carry her, and it worried him.

It must've shown on his face because she said, "Stop thinking like that. I'm going to make it through this."

He nodded.

"I'm not just saying that to make you feel better. I feel it in my bones that I'm going to make it through this just fine. I'm sure I'll have to wade through a lot of tough days along the way, but I'll make it to the other side of this challenge."

He could see the truth of her words in her expression.

He set her gently on her bed. Aiden leaped onto the bed and pulled the covers over his mom, making sure to tug it over her shoulders, straightening it out like it wasn't his first time. "You all comfy, momma?"

"Yes, because you're so good at this." He grinned, and she gave him a hug.

Jack turned to leave, but Rachel said, "No, stay. I'm exhausted, not sleepy. Tell me about work."

He nodded and took a seat in the chair near her bed. "Well, December's always super busy, of course, since that's when everyone wants to advertise the most. Many of the companies we work with have had their ad campaigns in the works for months, and we're just in the final stages of actually running the campaigns.

"We still have smaller companies coming to us last minute, though, looking for smaller campaigns to be thrown together quickly. But I've got a good team, and they handle the extra work well."

"You've done great things with your company. I'm proud of you."

"Thank you." Jack didn't have parents—Rachel had taken over that role when they'd both died when he was fifteen. So hearing that from her made his chest swell. He guessed it would've felt the same as if it had come from a parent.

Then she asked the question about work that he'd known she'd most wanted to hear about when she first asked. "And how is Noelle?"

He looked down, shaking his head, but still smiling just at the mention of her name. "She's good. Like always."

“When are you going to get around to asking her out already?”

He took a deep breath. She knew the answer—she’d asked the question plenty of times. “Still never. Because I’m still her boss.”

Jack had a good friend and an acquaintance who each dated employees in businesses they owned, and neither turned out well. His friend’s relationship had created a lot of office drama that really caused problems for the better part of a year. His friend had been lucky.

For his acquaintance, there had been office drama, indeed. But the bigger problem had been a bad breakup that caused cascading issues that had eventually brought his entire company down. Jack had eight employees whose livelihood depended on his company staying strong and doing well, and he felt the weight of that responsibility exquisitely.

“Such a shame.” She turned to her son. “Aiden, why don’t you get your snowflake collection to show Uncle Jack?” Aiden hopped off the bed. “Make sure you gather all the ones you made, not just the ones in the box. Get the ones on your bed and on the kitchen table and counters. Coffee table, too.”

Rachel watched the door until Aiden was out of sight, then turned to Jack. “I have a favor to ask.”

“Anything.”

“I want you to take Aiden to do Christmassy things this season.”

“Okay, ask me for anything but that.”

She swatted him on the arm. "I'm serious, Jack!"

"Come on, Rach. You know I'd do anything for you. But Aiden doesn't need a Grinch making him hate Christmas, too. I can't think of anyone who would be worse at it than I would."

"He needs this. I want him to have the kind of Christmases that we never had."

"And you've been giving it to him every year. One Christmas isn't going to make or break his feelings about Christmas."

"So, what..." She raised an eyebrow. "It takes an entire childhood of going without it to turn someone into a Christmas-hating Grinch?"

"Pretty much."

"Five years old is the most magical age to experience Christmas, and I don't want him missing out on that just because I'm sick." She paused for a long moment, then added, "Jack, it's important to me."

November and December were his busiest months at work, and he had to put in so many hours a week during those months to accomplish all that he needed to. But how could he say no to his sister's request? Especially when it was important to her?

He took a deep breath. "Okay, I'll make sure he experiences a fun Christmas." He couldn't guarantee it'd be him helping Aiden, but he'd make sure Aiden didn't miss out on a single thing.

She gave him a weak smile. "Thank you."

When Aiden came back into the room, his arms wrapped around a box that was almost too wide for his five-year-old arms, Rachel said, "I need to rest for a bit. Why don't you have Uncle Jack help you hang those up?"

Aiden nodded, and they both left the room, pulling the door closed behind them. Aiden set the box on the coffee table, then went to the kitchen and returned a moment later with a spool of kite string, a roll of tape, and a pair of scissors. After setting them down, he headed back to the kitchen, grabbed one of the chairs at their small table, and hefted it into the family room area.

"Mom says we can't put up the Christmas decorations until she's feeling a bit better, but we can put up these."

Jack hadn't even noticed that they didn't have decorations up. His lack of prickliness at first walking into the room should've tipped him off to their absence.

Aiden patted the stack of snowflakes he'd made from cutting folded paper. "I've been making these for a really long time. I'm talking for a really long time. Like, at least ten days. I want to hang them from the ceiling so it'll look like it's snowing in here. I know they aren't really Christmas decorations, but there's always snow at Christmas, so it's kind of like Christmas decorations."

He much preferred thinking of them as simply a winter thing.

They cut lengths of string, taped one end to each snowflake, and then Jack climbed onto the chair to tape them to the ceiling. Aiden started singing a song he was making up as they went along about hanging them up.

Jack was having fun. He liked hanging out with his nephew.

But then Aiden said, "I know! We should be listening to Christmas music instead of me singing!"

And then his nephew turned on the music, and a song about jingle bell time being a swell time filled the room, and Jack felt his hackles rise. The longer they worked and the more Christmas songs played, the more Grinch-like Jack could feel himself becoming. He just had too many negative feelings attached to Christmas from his childhood to ever enjoy the season again.

He taped a snowflake string to the ceiling, and Aiden said, "It needs to go that direction like this much." He held his hands about six inches apart.

"It's fine where it is," Jack snapped.

He immediately regretted the words, even before seeing Aiden's reaction to being barked at.

"Aiden, I'm sorry. I shouldn't have spoken sharply—that had nothing to do with you. It needs to go this direction, you said?" He pulled the tape from the ceiling and moved it to the right. Aiden nodded, so he stuck it in the new spot.

There was no way he could be the one to help Aiden experience the joy of Christmas. Jack couldn't be around anything relating to Christmas without feeling cranky, and no matter how hard he could try to hide it, it was bound to rub off on Aiden. He could never do the holiday justice for a five-year-old who was so wide-eyed and expectant of the season.

He needed to find help.

CHAPTER THREE

Noelle

Noelle sat around the conference table in the marketing meeting with her boss and her seven coworkers, talking about the ad campaigns they had running for clients and new ad campaigns they had coming up, taking notes about everything that had to do with her job as the copywriter. Assignments were made, deadlines were given.

And then, at the part where her boss, Jack, who was standing with his tablet in his hand, would typically wrap up the meeting by asking if anyone had any questions, he shifted from one foot to the other and then glanced down at the tablet. Then he placed it on the table and looked out at them, putting his hands in his pockets and looking a little uncomfortable.

The uncertain body language seemed out of place for a boss who was always very professional and businesslike and instantly made everyone pay a little more attention.

"I need some help outside of work for a project unrelated to work, and I'm wondering if any of you might be interested in the job. You would be paid—"

Noelle's hand shot into the air.

Jack glanced at her, pausing his sentence only momentarily before forging on. "—time and a half, and it would be eight to ten hours a week until the end of the month."

Noelle raised her arm as high as it would go as her brain started doing the math without her even telling it to. That would probably be everything she needed to get her car fixed, and it wouldn't involve working in a retail environment that would practically be exploding with Christmas. If that wasn't a giant Christmas miracle dropped right at her doorstep, she didn't know what was.

Winter miracle, she mentally corrected herself. Fortune smiling down on her. Divine intervention.

It would be so nice to drive her car again!

"Okay," Jack said, nodding at Noelle, "it looks like we have one person interested. Is anyone else?"

Noelle looked around the conference table. A couple of people looked thoughtful, but most looked uninterested or maybe even overwhelmed with work and the holidays. Lennox looked like he was considering it for a moment, then changed his mind. Bridget seemed to turn her nose up at just the thought of working more hours. She could probably put her arm down. Jack got that she was very interested.

"And that was our last item of business. Noelle, do you want to come to my office, and we'll talk more about the job?"

As she grabbed her stuff and walked to his office, her mind ran with possibilities of what the job might be. It wasn't spending extra time doing her regular job—he'd made that clear. It couldn't really be organizing files or anything like that, either, since he said it was unrelated to work. Whatever it was, overtime pay was something she couldn't pass up.

Why was it that walking into Jack's office made her feel like she was being "called on the carpet?" It was a funny expression, mainly because most of the building was carpeted, but Jack's office wasn't. His was modern and sleek, like it belonged in a magazine. A couch sat on one side, which should've made the place feel homier, but it didn't. It was leather with angled lines, and even though it had a small rug in front of it, even the carpet had clean lines and a short pile.

Poster-sized images of award-winning ads they had created hung framed on the walls, along with the awards, scaled to the same size. The only personal item in the room was a framed picture on his desk, but it faced him, not the side of the desk she was on. She always wished she had the guts to pick it up and look at it—to get a glimpse into what was important enough to him to be the only thing he deemed worthy of entering his workspace.

Everything was neat and tidy and organized, too, which was so at odds with their work in a creative business. No one else's desks here looked so orderly. It made her uncomfortable. Out of her element.

"Have a seat," he said as he shut the door behind her and went around to sit at his desk.

She took a seat on the leather chair, which, for the record, wasn't soft, even though it was padded. How she hadn't totally blown her interview in this same room a year and a half ago was beyond her. She'd felt just as out of place back then.

It didn't help that her boss was intimidatingly good-looking. He had those strong shoulders that looked so incredible in a suit. In the few times she'd seen him just wearing a dress shirt without the jacket, they'd looked even more impressive. Dark hair, dark eyes, strong jawline—he had it all.

Anyone would agree that he was a very beautiful man. But he had a stiff exterior that hid what he was like on the inside, and he never cracked. They all knew what kind of a boss he was—a very fair one—but no one knew what he was like outside of work, and he never gave any clues.

"I'm going to cut right to the chase here, Ms. Allred. My sister has Acute Myeloid Leukemia."

Noelle gasped.

"She's convinced she'll make it through, but she's been going through the most intense part of treatment right now and is pretty sick. She has a five-year-old son—my nephew, Aiden. Do you have any experience with kids?"

Her brows drew together. Was he looking for a babysitter? Why would he ask work colleagues for that kind of help when he could go to a site or app for caretakers? She hesitated. "I do. I have nine nieces and nephews. Two of them are five-year-old boys."

He nodded. "Good. My sister said that Christmas is a magical time for five-year-olds, and she doesn't want him to miss out on any of it just because she's sick. She asked for assistance in providing him with a magical Christmas. What I would need you to do is to help give that to him."

Noelle immediately stood. "I'm sorry; I can't."

Jack looked shocked by the abrupt ending of the negotiation. He stood, too. "Why? Is the pay not good enough for something like that? I can offer you more."

"It's not that. I just can't."

He cocked his head slightly. "I assure you, Noelle, that my nephew's a good kid."

"I am sure that he is. But I'm sorry—my answer is no." She didn't want to turn down something that had seemed like such a gift and an answer to all her problems. But there was no way possible that she could do what he was asking. And the longer she stayed in this room, the more he would think he might be able to talk her into it. "Now, if you'll excuse me, I've got a lot of work waiting for me."

Then she turned and walked out of his office, not even glancing back to see the look on her boss's face. She had always prided herself on being the one willing to take on any extra work whenever he asked, so her response was probably rather unexpected for him.

She really did have a lot of work to do before the end of the day, so she got herself in the ad copy mindset and focused deeply. She started with the copy for a group of ads showing the "perfect" stocking stuffers, and she was on fire. Sometimes, coming up with the right words to go with an ad image felt like an uphill climb when the hill was covered in thick molasses, making each step exhausting work. But other times, like today, the words came like running downhill with a breeze at her back.

After an hour of working so focused on the ads, she could feel her brain power waning, so she took a break to work on other tasks and give her creative juices time to recharge. She refilled her water bottle, sat back down, got comfortable, nudged some papers aside to make room for her water, then opened her email. The top one was from her boss, with a subject line that read *Extra hours*. She sighed and clicked on it.

Noelle,

I sincerely think that you're the best person for the job to help my sister and nephew. I really hope you'll reconsider.

Jack

Nope. That wasn't going to happen. She was super bummed that it wouldn't work out, but it very much wouldn't. So she clicked *reply* and typed, *I am sorry. I really wish I could help you, but I can't.* Then she clicked *send* and forced herself to work on writing ad copy for their "Gifts for the guy who has everything" campaign.

All through the rest of the afternoon, though, working *didn't* help her forget about Jack's request. Not only about how badly she needed the money or how much she just couldn't make herself do anything Christmassy to get it, but also about the pleading look that had been on her boss's face when he had asked. This was his company, and he was passionate about it. That had come through in so many staff meetings over the year and a half she'd worked there. She had seen plenty of impassioned pleas for them to pour their heart into specific projects or to put in extra hours when they had too many great clients needing their services at the same time.

His plea for his nephew had been different. It wasn't that it had been more sincere—that wasn't it. He was sincere about everything he did. She couldn't quite put her finger on what the difference was, though.

Regardless of what had been on his face, the fact remained that she couldn't do what he was asking. It just wasn't possible.

So it felt even worse when she got a text from Jack after she'd left work for the day, just as she was walking from the office to the bus stop.

> JACK: You have now mentioned twice that you "can't" help my nephew—never that you don't want to. Can I assume that means that there's an obstacle standing in your way that you can't get around? Is there something that I can do to help overcome the obstacle?

Noelle wasn't even sure how to respond. Could she pretend that she hadn't seen the text and answer once she had time to think about how to reply? Yeah, probably not—her phone was set to show when she'd read a message. She really needed to change that. She took a deep breath and clicked reply, then just dumped out her thoughts.

> NOELLE: It's more of a mental obstacle than a physical one. Although I did just slip on ice and slide my car into a pole, ruining the front corner just enough to make it un-driveable, so I guess it's also a physical one.

> NOELLE: But really, the far biggest issue of the two is the mental obstacle. So, no, there's not much you can do.

She touched send, then had a moment of freaking out that she just told her boss that she had mental obstacles. And suddenly, she couldn't handle seeing what his response might be to a declaration that was far more personal than she had ever been with her boss. Even admitting that she was having car troubles was out of the ordinary. So she hurried and shut her phone off before his response could come in and pushed her phone into her bag.

Then she reached in and pushed it further to the bottom. Underneath everything. Where a response wouldn't feel like it was trying to break free. But then she felt the metaphorical weight of the phone, which now only had the faux leather of her bag between it and her lap, so she moved the bag to the empty seat next to her.

She got off the bus, made the walk back to her apartment—on sidewalks now shoveled clear of snow, thankfully—and went into her apartment before she looked at her bag, trying to decide if she wanted to take her phone out of it and turn it back on.

It was the fact that she knew Hope would be calling that made her grab the phone and power it on. She didn't want to go to the event tonight, but she did love her sister.

No missed calls from Hope yet, which was unusual. But there were definitely two texts from Jack. She realized that she'd forgotten to get her mail, so she grabbed her keys and headed back down to the mail room, looking at the phone as she went, trying to work up the courage to swipe on the notifications. She unlocked her mail box, then hovered her finger over the messages for a long time before mumbling, *You're being a wimp*, then swiped to open the texts. She looked down at the phone in one hand, grabbing her mail with the other.

> JACK: I will pay for the repairs on your car. And while it's in the shop, I'll get you a rental to drive. As far as the mental obstacle, I don't know if I can do anything for that, but I'm hoping this will help…

The following text was just two pictures. The first was of a young boy who she guessed was his nephew. He looked like he was about five years old and was holding a snowflake cut from folded white paper, grinning at the camera. He was adorable, and she found herself smiling back at him. He kind of reminded her of her nephews.

The second picture was the same boy, sitting on the lap of someone who looked frail and like she wasn't feeling well. She guessed it was Jack's sister. That one made her heart hurt.

But so did thoughts of doing Christmas stuff with the boy. So she swiped out of the app before closing and locking her mail box. She had no idea how to respond.

As she walked back up to her apartment, she pushed her phone into her pocket and started looking through the mail in her hand. A package sat on top of some bills and junk mail. It was slightly smaller than a book but also thicker. It was some kind of box wrapped in brown paper. It was addressed to her, but there wasn't a return address.

Curious, she turned it over to the backside but then quickly turned it back as her brain interpreted what her eye must've caught. The postmark was from North Pole, Alaska. She sucked in a breath, staring at the postmark with disbelief. For as long as she could remember, her Gran-gran would send her a letter "from Santa," and the postmark always said North Pole, Alaska. The home of Santa Claus.

She'd figured out that Santa wasn't real when she was seven (which was bound to happen with three older sisters who already figured it out but didn't do all they could to keep the secret from her because she wasn't the youngest). When she'd gotten the letter from Santa that Christmas, she'd announced to Gran-gran that she no longer believed in Santa.

Gran-gran had just smiled, winked, and said, "I'll never stop believing in the magic of Christmas."

And then, when Noelle was eight, a letter from Santa still came, still with a postmark from North Pole, Alaska. They still kept coming, in fact, every year since then. One even arrived "from Santa," postmarked by the North Pole post office last year. Noelle had received it just two days after Gran-gran's passing.

She was still holding her breath, like letting it out might disturb the magic, and the box would vanish. But then, suddenly and with all the speed she could muster, she ran up the three flights of stairs as fast as she could.

Her keys shook in her hands as she tried to unlock the door. But she finally got the key in and turned, opened the door, and raced to dump the rest of the mail on her table.

Then she grabbed a pair of scissors from her kitchen junk drawer, forced herself to take the time to remove her key from the front door and shut it, then she took slow, deep breaths and forced herself to be calm.

Ever so carefully, so she wouldn't damage the brown paper, she sliced into the tape just enough to break it and unfolded the wrapping.

Inside was a metal box, with her name painted in her gran-gran's fancy handwritten script across the top. She ran her fingers across it reverently, like it was made of the most precious gems.

Maybe this was nothing. Maybe her parents knew she would struggle this Christmas, so they sent something to the North Pole post office to have it postmarked and sent back to Noelle.

But somehow, she knew it wasn't. With trembling fingers, she lifted off the top of the box.

Inside was a stack of cards on thick cardstock. She picked up the first one—it was a scene painted with watercolors of the tree lighting in Downtown Park. She recognized Gran-gran's style immediately. And among the people painted in the scene, she recognized Gran-gran by the red coat she always wore. Noelle stood next to her. She turned the card over and saw Gran-gran's flowing script that had gotten the tiniest bit shaky over the years.

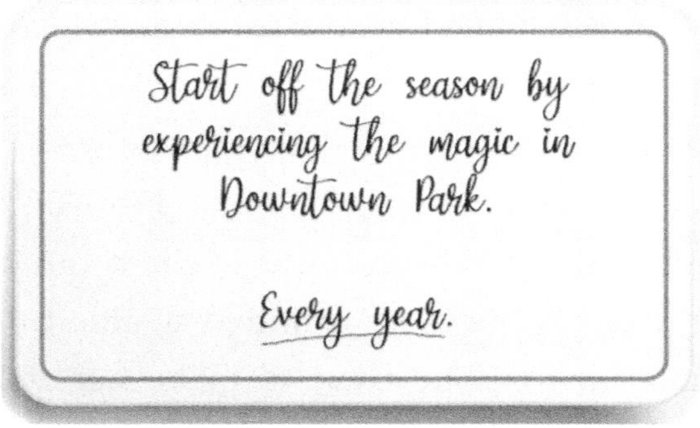
Start off the season by
experiencing the magic in
Downtown Park.
Every year.

She laughed once, covering her mouth with one hand, tears starting to fall from her eyes and run down her cheeks. Noelle's entire family always went to the tree lighting, but she and Gran-gran always stuck together like glue while they were there. All that magic she'd ever experienced in Downtown Park had been with her.

One by one, she went through the stack of at least a dozen cards. Each one had a scene painted of one of the traditions they did together, with the description written ever so carefully on the back. Each one of them said *Every year* at the bottom. She could feel her Gran-gran's presence with them all. She swiped at the tears that were running freely down her cheeks so they wouldn't fall onto the cards.

The pain of missing Gran-gran stabbed at her, but it was somehow a blunted stab this time. She could feel her presence with every card. Almost like she was with her as she looked at them.

She got to the last card, but there was no note or letter at the bottom. Where had these come from? And how did they get mailed from the North Pole a year after Gran-gran's passing?

Picking up her phone and dialing Hope with one hand, she picked up each card again, looking it over, overcome by the feeling that Gran-gran was in the room with her.

"Hello?" Her sister's voice sounded strained.

"Whatcha up to?" She tried to make her voice sound normal and happy.

"Wrangling kids into their car seats before we head over to the tree lighting." Noelle couldn't entirely trust her voice to come out normal. When she didn't immediately respond, Hope said, "Are you okay, Noe?"

Noelle nodded, then sniffed. "I got a package from Gran-gran."

"You—" Then, with her voice sounding further away from the phone, she said, "Honey, will you get this?" Then she was back. "You got a package? From Gran-gran? How?"

"I don't know. Hope, I need you to be one hundred percent truthful with me. Did you send this?"

"No."

"Do you know who did?"

"No. How? How did you get a package from Gran-gran?"

"I don't know. It's a metal tin containing cards she painted."

"And you're sure they're from her?"

"I'm sure." She looked at a card that showed Noelle and Gran-gran shopping for Christmas presents together. "She was definitely the one who painted these."

"But how did they get to you?"

Noelle shrugged again, even though she knew that Hope couldn't see it. "They came from North Pole, Alaska."

Hope gasped. "I want to see these. We've got to get to the tree lighting soon. Can I come over after I get the kids to bed?"

Noelle told her yes and ended the call, then just stood for a long time at her kitchen table, staring at the impossible cards and the words *Every year* at the bottom of each one. It was like she came back to give her a message. Like she knew just how badly she needed it.

After a long moment, Noelle wiped the tears from her cheeks and picked up her phone. Then she took a deep breath and went into Jack's message and touched the picture of Jack's nephew, enlarging it to the size of her screen. Then she swiped to the following picture of the boy and his mom.

She looked back at the box of cards. Did Gran-gran know that Noelle would quit Christmas once she was gone, and this was her way of making sure that didn't happen? Because the message seemed clear that Gran-gran still wanted all their traditions to happen every year, regardless of whether she was present or not. Like she knew that Noelle, specifically, needed to continue the traditions.

She rubbed her nose. Did her gran-gran somehow know that there was a little boy who needed her to do it, too?

Could she do it? What if she felt the pain of Gran-gran's absence so strongly every time she tried to do the things on the cards?

Maybe there was only one way to find out. She picked up her phone and texted Hope.

> NOELLE: Will you swing by and pick me up on your way to the tree lighting? But don't judge the state of my face.

Then, without even glancing in the mirror to see the damage done to her makeup and exactly how red and puffy her eyes and nose were from the crying, she grabbed her coat and keys and headed downstairs to meet her sister and her family.

CHAPTER FOUR

Jack

Jack thanked the man he'd been talking to on the phone, assured him that he'd be in touch soon to give him a detailed advertising plan, and hung up. The man owned a small business that made miniature games that were perfect for stocking stuffers, and he needed a last-minute Christmas campaign. Jack's company catered to small businesses who weren't big enough to have their own marketing department, so he was used to getting last-minute panicked requests for help.

Still, though, most years didn't usually have nearly this many last-minute calls.

He finished typing his notes about the company's needs and budget, added them to their list of projects for the month, added them to the agenda for the team meeting later, then pushed his notepad aside and ran his hands through his hair.

And then, because it had been so close to the front of his mind ever since the meeting yesterday, he started thinking about how he'd asked Noelle to help his nephew experience Christmas. The panic he'd been feeling ever since Noelle had sat in his office and turned down his request was returning in full force, too.

He worried that he wouldn't be able to find anyone else to help. And, really, he didn't *want* anyone else to help. He would be entrusting his nephew—his favorite little guy on the planet—with this person, so he needed to know and trust them. And in his gut, he knew that Noelle was the best option.

Plus, he'd talked to Rachel about Noelle enough that he knew Rachel would trust her, too, even though they'd never actually met. He hoped he hadn't been totally out of line by asking her to reconsider more than once, but he'd been desperate. He assumed he had been, especially since Noelle never texted back after he'd sent pictures last night.

He glanced at the clock on his wall—ten minutes to nine. He needed to catch Noelle as soon as she came into the office today and apologize for his unprofessionalism. He always worked hard to keep his attraction to her a secret because he was her boss, which meant that a relationship with her was utterly impossible.

Yet, he'd let himself cross that line of professionalism just because he cared about his nephew. He needed to rein it in. To come up with a Plan B. He never should've gone to any of his employees with a request that was so personal. Just because they were the people he knew the best and cared about and trusted the most was no excuse.

Especially because he'd already known that the line of professionalism was most challenging to keep with Noelle. She wore all of her emotions on her sleeve, so it was easy to tell how she was feeling at any given moment. And, with the singular exception of being tight-lipped about why she didn't want to help out with Christmas, she was usually pretty free with her thoughts and opinions and fears, doubts, hopes, everything.

She didn't seem to have much of a line at all. When he'd first hired her, he hadn't liked that she didn't just keep things professional. But over time, he'd grown to love it. It had helped him to get to know her so much better than he'd have ever gotten to otherwise.

But that was precisely why it was a problem. She made him feel comfortable around her. Like they were friends when they very much were not. So sometimes, he forgot there was a line. Like last night, when he'd texted her, begging for help. *Twice.* They were boss and employee, and that was all they could ever be. It was virtually the only thing he didn't like about being the boss.

But it wasn't like he could just do everything his sister hoped he would do all by himself. Not only was this his busiest month of the year, but he didn't have the slightest clue how to help Aiden with Christmas. A happy, "full" Christmas wasn't something he'd ever experienced himself. Rachel might as well have asked him to build a rocket ship and hop in it with Aiden and go show him the universe.

He glanced at the clock again. It was still several minutes before nine, but Noelle usually arrived a few minutes early. It was time to go apologize. He put his hands on his desk and was just standing when she appeared in his doorway. Her blonde hair was the perfect amount of curly, and she was wearing an ice blue blouse with navy jeans, ankle boots that he loved on her, and dangly silver earrings that brought out the sparkle in her eyes.

No smile this time, though, which was unusual for her. He had definitely crossed a line yesterday. She held a single piece of paper, and he really hoped it wasn't a resignation letter.

"Listen, Noelle. I need to apologize for—"

"Did you find anyone?"

The question—and the interruption—took him by surprise. He looked down, moved a paper on his desk with a single finger, then he put his hands in his pockets and met her eyes. "No. I've still been hoping that you'll take the job."

He couldn't believe he had just said that since he'd already decided against it. It was the concerned uncle side of him speaking, and he shouldn't have let it take over.

Noelle took another step into his office and closed the door behind her. "Okay, I'm just going to lay it all out here, even though it makes me feel awkward. But there are conditions, and you need to know them before accepting my help."

She might still be willing to help? He held his breath, waiting to hear more.

"My gran-gran died a year ago, and she was the most important person in the world to me. Everything Christmas-related I did with her, so everything about Christmas is now entwined with missing her. I didn't want to have anything to do with Christmas without her here, but apparently, she has other plans for me."

Other plans? He raised an eyebrow. He was curious but didn't want to say anything, afraid it might make her stop talking.

"I need to know why you don't want to do this yourself. You clearly love your nephew."

He gave his standard answer. "I don't have time."

"And?"

He should've known that she'd see right through him. And that she'd be okay crossing the line to push for a deeper answer. But he wasn't about to share the whole tale of his childhood, so he was going to keep his response short. He cleared his throat. "Growing up, Christmas wasn't a happy time of the year at my house. I don't know how to make it different for Aiden."

Noelle studied him for a long moment, and he wondered what she was seeing. She didn't seem to be judging him, though. She just seemed curious. He thought he was keeping his face relatively impassive, but judging by her expression, she was seeing more than he meant to show.

She stepped forward and placed the paper on his desk. He didn't dare take his eyes off her to look at it.

"Okay, I'll do this under one condition. I decide what we're going to do. It'll be stuff Aiden will love, of course. And I'll be all 'Happy, happy Christmas' around Aiden, even if I'm not feeling it, but you need to be that way, too, even if you're not feeling it. I'll plan everything and get anything we'll need, which will ease the time commitment on your part and take away your worries that you don't know what to do to give him a good Christmas." She pointed at the paper. "That's the schedule, and I expect you to be present for at least half of the events."

He liked this commanding side of her. He kind of wished that she was like this all the time. He picked up the paper and glanced at it. There were half a dozen things listed, along with specific dates of when they would happen.

His eyes flew back to hers. "Some of these things are in Mountain Springs. Is that where you live?"

She nodded.

"That's where my sister and my nephew live."

She smiled—the first one he'd seen from her since she walked in. He looked back down at the list, his brow crinkling.

"There are family things on this list. *Your* family things." He wasn't sure what he thought of that. Would it be awkward for Aiden to be with a family he didn't know? Would it be awkward for Jack, as well, since he would be required to attend most of these outings, too?

"My family is big and welcoming and crazy about Christmas. In the extreme. My dad, in particular, would keep Christmas decorations up year-round if he could. And they like to celebrate *big*. It'll be the perfect place for Aiden to experience Christmas." She nodded at the list. "Those are my conditions, and the things on the list aren't negotiable."

He glanced through the list again. "The final say is up to my sister, Rachel, since Aiden is her kid, but as far as I'm concerned, we have a deal."

Noelle smiled big and held out a hand, so he shook it.

"Okay, but get an answer soon because the first one on the list happens tomorrow at two."

He managed to hold off the smile threatening to overtake his face until she turned on her heel and walked out his door.

CHAPTER FIVE

Noelle

Noelle went back to her desk, let out a huge breath of relief, and collapsed into her chair, sinking into the backrest. She wasn't confrontational or demanding, so she was pretty proud of herself for pulling that off with her boss. But it had been exhausting.

Bridget was just setting her things down on her desk for the day and looked down at her watch. "It's nine oh one. It's way too early to be that tired. Especially on a day when we've got to make something like *Lump of Coal Breath Mints* sound like a good stocking stuffer."

Noelle laughed and sat up in her chair like normal. "It's days like today where we really get to prove how good we are at our jobs." And that was one of the reasons why she loved her job. How boring would it be to work at a big ad agency where they only had to make things like jewelry and sweaters sound like good gifts?

She opened her bag and pulled out the metal box she'd gotten from Gran-gran, placing it on her desk, right in front of her keyboard. Then she took off the lid and pulled out the card she'd already placed on top of the stack—the one with the little painting of the two of them making a snowman in Downtown Park.

And, really, today wasn't a *bad* day. For starters, it was Friday. She put the card, snowman painting facing forward, leaned against her monitor. As long as Jack's sister was on board with her's and Jack's Christmas pact —and the expression on his face told her that he thought she would be—she was going to get Elfie fixed, and she was going to honor Gran-gran's wishes. It might not be the easiest way to do either, but she at least had a plan and having a plan felt good.

On Saturday afternoon, she pulled up to the address that Jack had texted her—the address to his sister Rachel's house. He'd kept his word. She was driving a rental car, and he'd told the shop to charge him for the repairs.

As she walked up to the small home, she decided that the Grinch-ness that Jack had must not be a family thing, because it looked like Rachel had quite a few Christmas decorations and lights outside her house.

Jack answered the door, wearing a dark gray t-shirt and jeans. For the record, he looked every bit as amazing in jeans and a t-shirt as he did in a suit. But it was so strange seeing him not dressed up for work. It was a peek into his personal life that she hadn't seen before, and it felt wrong. Like looking through the pictures on someone's phone without permission or going trick-or-treating as a kid and knocking on the door of a house that you didn't realize belonged to your teacher.

A young boy wearing socks but no shoes came racing down the hall—Aiden, she assumed—with a golden retriever at his side. He skidded to a stop on the hardwood floor and held out a hand, beaming, like he was proud of himself for knowing how to greet someone for the first time. "Hi. I'm Aiden. And this is Bailey."

Noelle shook his hand. "Hello, Aiden." She nodded at the dog. "Bailey. It's nice to meet you both."

Jack closed the door behind her. "Come meet my sister." He put his hand on the small of her back just long enough to give a gentle nudge toward the hallway, and the touch sent an unexpected thrill up her spine.

She walked down the hallway with him, Aiden skipping ahead of them, toward a combined kitchen, dining room, and family room. His sister sat in a recliner in the modest room, looking even sicker than she had in the picture Jack had sent. But she was smiling and looked happy as they walked to her.

"Rachel, this is Noelle. Noelle, this is my sister, Rachel."

Rachel reached out both hands and enveloped her hand. "Thank you for coming. It's so good to meet you! Jack has told me a lot about you."

Jack flinched like he was panicked that his sister shared that. But why would he care? Of course, he would tell his sister about Noelle. She would be hanging out with her son a lot over the next few weeks—Rachel would naturally want to know about her.

They chatted for a few minutes while Aiden pulled on his snow boots, coat, hat, and gloves, then he and Jack drove to Downtown Park in his car, and Noelle drove in her rental. She made it out of her car and to the sidewalk in front of the park first, holding a couple of square buckets that she'd found handy for whatever sculpture they made. The sun was shining brightly, making everything look crisp and new and not nearly as cold as it actually was.

People were standing on the sidewalks and on the pathways they'd shoveled in the park itself, waiting for the event to start. They'd had a good snowstorm earlier in the week and a second one last night. The weather had been a little warmer for both, so the snow was nice and good for packing. Some years it had been so cold that the snow was nothing but powder, which was great if you were skiing, not so great if you were trying to make a snowman.

She spotted her sister, Hope, with her family and waved. She could see her sisters Becca and Julianne with their families, too, and her youngest sister, Katie, with her parents. Seeing them just made all the memories of being at this event over the years flood back in. Of course, the memories included all the family she saw here, but she and Gran-gran always worked on the same snow sculpture even if the rest of them didn't, so her memories included her, especially.

Right out in the middle of the park, they'd created a canoe one year. It looked like it was floating on the snow, and they'd made a snowman inside holding two big sticks like they were oars going down into the snow. And over by the nativity, they'd once made two dozen snowmen that were each about a foot and a half high with little black circular rocks for the eyes and a little bigger one for a mouth, all looking like they were a choir singing. One year, they'd even made a sculpture of a person making a snow angel.

And the whole time, Gran-gran had made jokes, and they'd laughed until their guts hurt, and Gran-gran made her feel like the most important person in the world.

She could feel her emotions rising as she saw Jack and Aiden get out of Jack's car and start heading in her direction, so she tamped them down. It had sounded like a good idea to follow Gran-gran's wishes and still celebrate Christmas when she'd gotten the cards and when Jack had been asking for help, but now that she was actually here, she was questioning that choice. There were just so many memories tied up in these activities that she wasn't sure she could do it.

But Aiden looked so cute, all decked out for the snow, and he had such a massive smile on his face. And Jack was looking pretty fine in his coat, gloves, and hat. More than fine.

She was taken aback by the thought. *He was her boss.* And not just a regular boss, but an "always keep things professional" boss. The kind that made you not even stop to consider how good-looking he was because it wouldn't be professional. But this wasn't the office, he wasn't wearing a tie, and somehow it made it so much easier to see just how attractive he was.

She cleared her throat as they neared. "So, Aiden, have you ever done this activity before?" He shook his head. "Everyone divides themselves into teams as small or as big as they want. When it's time to start, they say go, and then we've got forty minutes to make whatever we're going to make. After, we'll get hot chocolate in that gazebo that looks like a gingerbread house, then we can check out Santa's village."

She pointed toward the life-sized nativity. "Some people make animals around the manger." Then she motioned toward Santa's village with the train going around it. "Some people make elves or other Christmassy things over there. Some people make funny snowmen, and some people make things that don't really have anything to do with Christmas at all. One year, someone made a pretty impressive dragon. What do you think we should make?"

Aiden pondered it for a moment, tapping a finger on his lips, the most serious expression on his face. Then he raised his finger into the air. "I think we should make a chair."

Jack looked at Noelle, his eyebrows drawn together, then looked back at Aiden. "A chair?"

"Yeah, like a big, padded comfy chair that anyone can sit in. And we should put it right over there so whenever someone sits in it, they can look at everything. Oh, and we should have a snow dog that looks just like Bailey sitting up beside the chair. And there should be a footrest."

"You've got it, buddy." Jack chuckled and ruffled the big pom on the top of Aiden's hat like he was ruffling his hair, and it was definitely the cutest thing she'd seen all week. And she'd seen her six-year-old niece trying on her Mrs. Claus costume for her school play, so the competition had been tough.

They went and found a spot and chatted as they waited for the organizers to say it was time to start. She'd kept her focus mainly on Aiden and asking him questions, but since he liked to also answer for Jack, she'd found out that Jack loved playing Uno, hated the color brown, and wished there was a good Thai restaurant in Mountain Springs.

She'd also met Quinton, a dark-haired kid with a blue and orange coat who was one of Aiden's friends from school. The two had talked rather animatedly about what they were each going to make.

They started building the snow dog sitting tall on his hind legs first, scooping the snow with their arms and pulling it to where they needed it. After they made the general shape of the dog, they started shoveling the snow with their hands, pushing it into the dog, and the more they did, the more the blob of snow began to look like an actual dog. Jack seemed to know just how to press the snow in hard and smooth it out with his glove, using the tip of his gloved fingers to scrape in details. He might not have had a lot of experience with Christmas growing up, but he had clearly had a lot of experience playing in the snow.

And he was so good with Aiden. He showed him how to do all of the things and let Aiden take over so much of it. It was clear that Aiden adored his uncle, too. Doing things together like this didn't seem to be a foreign thing. Which was strange because with as professional and terse as Jack always was at work, she hadn't really pictured him being good with kids.

She hadn't pictured any of this, really. Not too far into making the comfy chair, they had to start filling the buckets to bring the snow from a little further out. The more they worked, the more she saw the mask of professionalism fall from Jack. He looked like he was actually enjoying himself. Truthfully, she hadn't known it was a mask.

He was laughing and joking with her, too.

She bit a finger of her glove to hold it as she pulled it off, then she took out her cell phone and snapped a few pictures of the two of them working. Purely for Rachel's and Jack's sake. Not that she was going to go home and stare at them and think about how very good-looking her boss was and how completely adorable he was with his nephew.

Not that she could allow herself to fall for him, though, no matter how attractive or adorable or funny or very not-stuffy he was. Even if he wasn't acting like her boss right now, he was still her boss. She hadn't seen or heard anything about coworkers not being able to date anyone they worked with, but no one had dated anyone from the office the whole time she'd worked there. That could've been at least partly because there was a small dating pool available, but even if it wasn't said, everyone probably assumed they couldn't just by having Jack as a boss. It seemed like the kind of thing he wouldn't be okay with.

As they neared the end of the time limit and, thankfully, the end of their project, Jack kept stopping to take his phone out of his pocket, frown at it, and then type something. She knew he hadn't wanted to be there at all, so a part of her wondered if he was just laying the groundwork for skipping out early. He would probably break the news by saying there was some kind of emergency and was working on making it more believable.

"Alright, buddy," Jack said. "I think it's time you tested this chair out to see how it feels."

Aiden sat down in the chair made of snow, his arms on the armrests, sitting in it like a king sitting in his throne, then put his feet up on the little ottoman they'd made, and he leaned back and surveyed the park and everything going on in it. He reached out and put a hand on the snow dog's head beside the chair, giving him a little pat.

Then, with an entirely satisfied look on his face, he declared, "We did good work."

Both she and Jack smiled at the cute boy. It felt good to see him so proud of his idea come to life.

Then, just as they blew the whistle to stop, Jack pulled the phone out again and frowned at it. Then he put it back into his pocket and bent down to Aiden's height. "Listen, buddy. I've got to go."

"But we haven't gone around to see what everyone made yet. And we haven't gone on the train around Santa's village."

"I know, and I'm sorry. Do you want to stay with Noelle and do those things?"

Aiden looked up at Noelle and smiled, nodding enthusiastically as he turned back to Jack. "But I'm still sad you have to go."

"I'm sad, too. I'll make it up to you, okay?"

Then Jack stood up, and as the righteous indignation that had been building inside her since he'd first started taking his cell phone out built to a crescendo, he said, "Are you okay to finish up here and take Aiden home after?"

Aiden's friend Quinton came over just then, excitedly talking about his family's creation, so she took the moment while he was distracted to pull Jack aside a bit. "So you're only sticking around for the wintery part and then coming up with an excuse to leave for the more Christmassy part of the event? You know, you're not the only person who is struggling with this."

Jack just looked at her, not saying a word, the muscle at his jaw clenching. She tried to stand tall and interpret the look on his face, but it was pretty impassive, and she was wincing inside pretty hard. She wasn't the kind of person who just stood up to her boss and told him that he was doing things wrong. She was the kind of person who got an assignment and did it cheerfully. She didn't know what had come over her.

Jack turned and left without a word.

She was the only one of them getting paid for being there—an amount per hour that she wouldn't be able to get anywhere else—so maybe she should quit her judging and silent complaining. And definitely quit the out loud complaining to him.

She put a smile on her face and held out a hand to Aiden. "Are you ready to go look at what everyone made?"

He put his hand in hers. "Yep. We need to start with Quinton's. They made a robot wearing a Santa hat!"

As they walked around and saw all the snow creations that had turned out great and the ones that hadn't turned out so great, she felt terrible. Not only from the myriad of memories of Gran-gran that caused a new wave of grief to wash over her but because she felt bad about how she'd spoken to Jack.

After Aiden had gone on the train, went with her all through the village to see all of the elves working hard to make presents and get them wrapped and loaded onto Santa's sleigh, then went on the train another two times, they took off their gloves and headed over to the gazebo to get hot chocolate. They had just gotten their cup of sweet and warm goodness, holding on to the curved part of a candy cane while they stirred the chocolate, when her phone buzzed.

She pulled it out of her pocket and saw that it was Jack. Probably calling to say that he didn't think it was appropriate for her to talk to him like that, which would be totally fair. She answered, and before he even had a chance to say anything, she said, "Jack, I need to apologize. I—"

"Are you two still at the park?"

"Yes."

"Good. My sister started doing a lot worse after we left, and I had to take her to the hospital. It's probably going to be several hours before we can leave."

Noelle's stomach dropped, and she felt even worse.

"I've spoken with the mom of his friend Quinton. Do you remember meeting him?" He was back to being Boss Jack, not Playful Jack.

"I do."

"Keep an eye out for her—they're going to take Aiden home with them. They'll stop by Rachel's and grab his bag, then he'll sleep over at their house. Can I speak to Aiden for a minute to let him know?"

She held the phone out to Aiden. He set his hot chocolate down on the ledge of the gazebo and cradled the phone in both hands as he held it to his ear. She couldn't hear what Jack was saying and only heard a long line of "Uh-huh. Uh-huh" coming from Aiden. Then, "And mommy will be okay?" followed shortly by, "Will she call to tell me goodnight before bed?" and "When will I get to see her?"

Her heart was breaking for the poor kid.

Then Aiden said, "Okay. I love you, Uncle Jack." Then he handed the phone back to Noelle. "He wants to talk to you."

She put the phone up to her ear and said, "I shouldn't have been so quick to judge you when I knew I didn't have the full story."

He was quiet for a long moment. She was about to pull the phone away from her ear to see if either she or Aiden had accidentally hung up when he said, "Keep calling me out whenever you think I'm not doing the right thing."

She was too dumbfounded to make actual words come out of her mouth but did manage to make a sound somewhat resembling an "Oh?"

"It's a skill not enough people utilize because they worry it might make someone mad. And it might do exactly that. But don't let it stop you."

"Um, okay." The word came out as more of a question than she'd intended.

"And Noelle?" His voice was lower than usual, and her name sounded different from how he normally said it.

"Yeah?"

"Thank you for staying with Aiden."

She hung up the phone and looked up at the ceiling of the gazebo, knowing that she was in trouble. She had worked for Jack for a year and a half and hadn't once gone home thinking thoughts about how attractive he was—inside or out. Yet, she knew she'd be going home thinking about him today.

And that was very bad.

CHAPTER SIX

Jack

Jack knocked on the door of what he was pretty sure was Noelle's parents' house in Mountain Springs. The address seemed right. So did the decorations. Although most homes in the neighborhood had Christmas lights on their houses and a tree or two, this house was, by far, the one decorated the most. Noelle had said that her family was enthusiastic about celebrating Christmas, but he still hadn't imagined it to this extent.

Lights outlined the house and windows and covered the dozen trees and shrubs in the front yard. The decorations rivaled the ones that had been in Downtown Park during the snow sculpture competition—the nativity and Santa's village both included.

Aiden ran through the snow and wrapped his arms around one of a set of three giant Christmas tree bulbs that were nearly as tall as him like he was giving it a hug. "Look at how big they are!"

Aiden stomped the snow off his feet as they walked to the front door and then knocked. A girl who looked like she was about seven years old answered and invited them inside. A black lab was at her side and gave a single bark of a welcome, and Aiden immediately reached out and pet his head.

The girl pointed to a living room that was just off the entryway and said, "You can put your coats in there."

They both shrugged off their coats and added them to the pile on the couch. Jack asked the girl for Noelle, and she said she was in the kitchen before skipping past a living room and into a family room he could see from the doorway.

They followed her and the dog and entered an area filled with people and Christmas decorations, Christmas music playing overhead. They were at the back of a family room that was open to a kitchen, with the most enormous dining room table he'd ever seen separating the two rooms. A twelve-foot tree rose to the ceiling in the family room, and about ten little kids played with toys in the open area in front of it.

A few adults were in the family room area, too, sitting on the couches holding a toddler or on the floor with the kids or standing, bouncing a baby. The rest of them were in the kitchen area, which was a hive of activity.

Aiden tugged on Jack's shirt, not taking his wide eyes off the rooms full of people, so Jack leaned down.

"*All* of these people are Noelle's family?" he whispered.

"I think so. I know she has four sisters, and I think three of them are married and have kids." There were definitely four people he could guess were her sisters in the kitchen, but six women were about the right age.

And, taking a quick count as he looked around, there were enough spouses for five people. So maybe there were more than just siblings here. There were literally a dozen little kids, from babies to possibly seven years old, and he saw a couple who were an age that he could only assume meant they were her parents.

"How did they get so many?"

"I don't know, buddy."

A pack of three kids, all boys, two who looked Aiden's age and one maybe a year younger, were building a tower out of something that looked like magnetic tiles. One of them got up and came over to Aiden. "Want to come play with us?"

Aiden looked up at Jack, and Jack nodded, so Aiden ran off to join them. One asked what his name was, and that was all it took for them to become friends. Aiden was helping them, a big grin on his face.

Noelle spotted Jack from where she stood in the kitchen and wiped her hands off on an apron she had tied around her waist as she made her way to him.

"Hi! I'm glad you could make it. Come on, let me introduce you to everyone." Then she grabbed him by the hand and pulled him past the family room and the dining table to where the bulk of the people were working on getting all the gingerbread parts ready in the kitchen, and he tried to ignore how it felt to have Noelle's hand in his.

"Hey, everyone, this is my boss, Jack. And that little guy over there playing with the boys is Aiden." Then, rapid-fire, she introduced everyone to him. He quickly caught her sister's names—Becca, Hope, Julianne, and Katie—since he'd heard them before, but the rest of the names were lost the moment she pointed to the next person and said their name. He did catch that two adult males were cousins, and two of the women she'd pointed at were their spouses. The names didn't stick, but he did remember which ones were sisters, and he kind of caught which spouses were married to each other.

"Oh, and while we're all here," Noelle said, "does anyone know anything about who sent me the box of Christmas activity cards that Gran-gran painted?"

Everyone shook their heads, a few with eyebrows raised, but they all looked like they didn't know what she was talking about.

"No? Come on. It had to be one of you. Sent to the post office in North Pole, Alaska first, to get the postmark?"

"Honey," her mom said, "you might just have to accept that you'll never find out how it got to you."

But Noelle swung around and pointed at the guy who he was pretty sure was married to Noelle's sister, Hope. "None of you are lying, right? Cory. You helped a lot in cleaning out Gran-gran's painting room. It was you, wasn't it?"

Cory held up both hands. "Noelle, I swear to you, if it had been me who had found a box she left with your name on it, I would've just handed it to you back in

January when we cleaned everything—I wouldn't have gone to the work of saving it for all these months and then shipping it to the North Pole first."

"Yeah, you totally would've. It was no one? Really?" Noelle sighed.

"It sounds like the verdict is in," Noelle's dad said, grinning as he looked around the room at everyone. "It's a Christmas miracle."

Everyone laughed, but Jack didn't quite understand why.

Noelle leaned into Jack. "Every Christmas season, my dad declares at least one thing—but sometimes up to a dozen things—a 'Christmas miracle.' It has pretty much become its own tradition now."

"All right," Katie said, clapping her hands together, "now that that's settled, who wants to be interviewed for our annual Christmas Eve video?"

One of Noelle's brothers-in-law raised his hand, and Noelle nodded toward the kitchen counter. "Want to help me fill icing bags?"

He nodded and followed her through the crowd of people, who had all gone back to doing whatever jobs they had been doing before they paused for introductions. Noelle lifted a big mixing bowl from the stand, placed it on the counter, and then used a rubber spatula to scrape around the edges. Then she pulled toward them a stack of triangular-shaped bags that he could only guess were made of silicone and lifted the top one from the pile.

"We just need to drop in one of the tips and make sure it's in the spot at the bottom just right, then we'll fill them maybe half full. Do you want to hold or fill?"

"Hold." Definitely. He didn't have a clue what they were doing.

So he held the bag open as she scooped a bunch of the frosting onto the rubber spatula and put it into the bag, kind of wiping it off against the edge of the bag. Then she went for a second scoop.

It was awkward work, and it required them to stand close enough that the sides of their bodies were touching, their arms trying to occupy the same space. He kept things very professional at work, so there had never been a situation where he'd been this close to her before, and he found her presence intoxicating.

She took the bag from him and moved her hands around the outside, probably trying to get the frosting in the right place, then twisted the top and added a clip to it. He picked up the next bag and put the icing tip into it, just like she'd shown him.

"How is Rachel doing?"

He looked over to meet her eyes, which were definitely green and not hazel. This close, he could see the facets in her eyes and the darker rim around the outside that was almost a navy blue. He'd always thought that her eyes were bewitching, but they were even more so when he was this close.

"She's doing okay. Much better than she was Saturday night or even yesterday." It had touched him that she had sought him out at work this morning to ask how she was doing after her hospital visit.

"That's good to hear. You must be worried about her all the time. I bet that's stressful."

It was. No one had ever really acknowledged that before. He hadn't even really acknowledged that stress—he'd only ever thought about the worry he had.

They continued to work, filling bags. On one, he must not have been paying enough attention to the bag because one side folded in just as Noelle was putting the icing in, getting it on the part of the bag that was supposed to be on the outside. They both jerked forward to fix it, and the rubber spatula got knocked out of Noelle's hand, which they both tried to catch. They managed to keep it from falling to the counter or the floor, but icing got on his hand, her arm, and a bit had taken to the air and landed on Noelle's cheek.

Noelle laughed and reached for a roll of paper towels, and he found himself chuckling. She pulled one off the roll and handed it to him. He cleaned off his hand, then got a second paper towel and said, "Here, let me get the part on your cheek."

He found himself holding his breath as he wiped the frosting from her skin, his face just inches from hers. And she seemed to be holding her breath, too, as whatever this was passed between them. A heat. A spark. A connection. Something. And he knew it wasn't just him who was feeling it.

He dropped his hand and set the paper towel on the counter as she cleared her throat and turned back to the icing bags.

All of the adults who weren't currently holding a child in their arms helped to get all the correct gingerbread pieces placed at each spot at the table, with the icing and candy for decorating spread evenly throughout. Then everyone started finding seats around the table. Jack and Noelle found a spot with Aiden right between them.

It was a bit overwhelming seeing so many family members around the big table. He was pretty sure his parents each had a sibling or two, but honestly, they had never talked about them. Neither of his parents had grown up with close families. It had only been the four of them until he was fifteen, and then it was just him and Rachel until Aiden was born. Aiden's father had never even been in the picture. So all of this? It was a little too much.

"I don't get how this makes a train car," Aiden said, holding up two rectangle pieces of gingerbread. "There aren't even any wheels."

"See that table over there?" Noelle pointed at a large side table against the far wall with a Christmas village set up. "There's a train track that goes all around it. The wheels are over there—what we're making looks kind of like a box. We'll put our gingerbread train cars on top of the wheels over there, and then the train can actually go around the track."

"Cool! And does this gingerbread man go inside it?"

Noelle smiled. "No. That's for you to decorate then take home and eat."

Jack watched Noelle help Aiden as he worked on his own train car. He loved how patient she was with his nephew and how well she explained how to make the box and helped hold some pieces but let him do all the parts he could do on his own. It was sweet. He knew Rachel couldn't give Aiden all the attention he needed right now and knew how happy it would make her to know her son was so well cared for. It made him happy, too.

Once they had their train cars made and were decorating them with the candy and icing, Aiden let out a long exhale. "I wish my mom was here making these, too."

Noelle set down her icing bag. "How about we take lots of pictures? Then you can tell her about every single bit of it when you get home and show her the pictures, and she'll feel like she was here."

Aiden nodded his head enthusiastically. Jack probably should've thought about taking pictures on his own. Noelle pulled out her phone and took a few pictures, then Aiden turned to Jack and tapped his arm. "You get some on your phone, too. Get a selfie with me, you, and Noelle."

Jack held his phone out to get all of them, but Aiden apparently wasn't happy with Noelle being the furthest away from the camera, so Aiden turned to Noelle and said, "Come over here and squish your face right between mine and Uncle Jack's."

Noelle's face reddened a bit, but she got out of her seat and positioned her face right between him and Aiden. Close enough that he could smell her peppermint shampoo and feel the buzz of energy that seemed to be fueled simply by their being so close.

When everyone finished their creations, they all headed over to the table with the Christmas village and placed their train cars on the mechanical wheel base set on the tracks. With his parents gone when he was fifteen, he'd always felt like he had to spend all of his extra time doing things that made money. Even after his company became profitable, he never slowed down to do something like this. He hadn't even felt like he should come to this activity tonight because there was so much more work to do back at the office. Noelle had only said that he had to be at half of the activities, so this had been one he had definitely planned to skip.

But after missing half of the last event, he decided that he didn't want Noelle thinking he couldn't keep his word. At least he was pretty sure that was his entire reason for coming tonight. Or maybe he just hadn't been willing to admit that other feelings about Noelle played a role in the decision. Regardless of the reason, tonight had felt refueling, somehow, which totally surprised him. He wouldn't have guessed that would be what he'd be feeling at this point.

Once everyone's train car was on the tracks, Noelle's dad turned the train on, and Aiden watched in wonder as the train went all around the village, carrying the train cars that they had just made.

Jack looked at Noelle, and they both shared a smile. But he knew that his smile wasn't just about seeing Aiden's wonder. It was also about Noelle herself. He'd already felt attracted to her more than he was okay with, but now he felt a deepening attraction to her that scared him.

This woman was going to be the death of him. She was as off-limits as they came since not only was she his employee, but she was currently his employee times two.

CHAPTER SEVEN

Noelle

Noelle sat down at her desk at work, and before she got started on the day's work, she pulled out her tin of cards from Gran-gran and started shuffling through them. When she came across the scene painted of the two of them making a snow creation in Downtown Park, she smiled and put it back in the tin. A little acknowledgment of having finished that part of what Gran-gran had wanted her to do.

Then she came across one of them decorating the boxcars for the gingerbread train. That one made her insides smile, too, just thinking about the look on Jack's face as he had moved in close to wipe the frosting off her cheek and the feeling—almost an electricity—that passed between them. Seeing him help Aiden was so sweet, too. She couldn't believe that she had worked with this man for a year and a half and hadn't had a clue about who he really was.

And now that she had caught a glimpse of it, she could feel herself falling for him. Which wasn't a good idea *at all*. But still, she'd take that smile he gave her as they saw

Aiden's face at seeing the train go around the Christmas village any day. All day, any day.

"Look at you being all smiley," Bridget said, and Noelle jumped, not even realizing that her coworker was at her desk, let alone watching her. "Dish. Tell me what's new in your life."

Noelle immediately thought of Jack, but she wasn't about to say anything about him to Bridget. Instead, she said, "I don't know. I guess it's just because I'm finding the Christmas spirit again after losing it a year ago."

"Aww! That's so sweet! Do you know who else is finding their Christmas spirit as well?"

"Who?"

"Our boss."

Noelle's eyebrows rose, and she glanced toward the hall that held Jack's office.

"Do you remember what a Grinch he was last year?" Bridget asked. "The biggest Grinch you've ever known, right? He always wants to work more at Christmas and gets even more surly whenever he sees Christmas decorations on people's desks and stuff like that."

"Oh." Noelle glanced back toward Jack's office. "I had just assumed that he had something hard going on in his life last year."

Bridget shook her head. "This is my third Christmas here—he's like that every year."

Lennox must've been listening in as he was typing something into his computer because then he swiveled his chair around their direction and said, "I can confirm that it's an every year thing. I don't know what's changed in his life, but I was the first person here this morning, and I actually heard him whistling a Christmas tune."

"No way," Noelle said.

Lennox shrugged. "I'm not even kidding you. But I know you won't fully believe it until you've checked it out for yourself."

She really did want to experience it because it made her insides flutter, just thinking that she maybe had something to do with it. The fact that he was changing his opinions about Christmas enough that other people were noticing was kind of a big deal. And, okay, her insides fluttered just thinking about Jack himself. So she grabbed her notebook and stood up.

She walked to just outside his office, still out of sight but close enough to hear if he was whistling. He wasn't; he was on the phone with someone, saying, "No, I haven't even had a chance to shop yet. This is our busy season, and I've been spending any extra time with Rachel and Aiden." There was a pause for a moment, then he said. "I know. I don't know why I'm procrastinating."

Now she just felt like an eavesdropper, so she turned to go back to her desk, but then just as quickly did a u-turn and headed to his open doorway.

He saw her and held up one finger, letting her know to stay and wait. Which she did while also scrambling to come up with a question to ask him to justify standing in his doorway with her notebook. She probably should've thought of that before leaving her desk.

He finished the call and then hung up. Then his eyes met hers, and he said, “Good morning. Did you need to talk to me?” His professional mask was back up. It had been almost jarring yesterday morning, after spending Monday evening with the real Jack, but today it just felt normal.

“Yes, I was looking at the info sheet for the Samurai blenders at Copperstone’s but didn’t see where it’s going to be advertised.”

“Oh. I apologize for missing that." He glanced at a paper on his desk. “Facebook, Instagram, Pinterest, and Google Ads.”

She nodded, wishing that she’d thought about grabbing a pen, too, so the notebook in her hands would actually have a use. She drummed her fingers on the back of the notebook, trying to decide if she wanted to ask him or not. Then she took a step forward.

“Did I hear you say that you haven’t done your shopping yet?”

Shopping was one of the activity cards that Gran-gran had painted. She’d had such a fun time decorating the gingerbread trains with him, so why not do the shopping one with him, too? She was just so drawn to him. Being around him had awakened feelings for him that she hadn’t known she had, and she was curious about just how strong those feelings were. And she really wanted to see more of what he was like outside of the office.

He nodded.

"Do you want to go shopping with me today? Maybe it won't seem like such a hurdle if we do it together."

It felt weird asking him that in the office since it was such a professional space, not a personal one. And this felt like a very personal ask. But they'd had so many personal moments over the past week that it also felt okay. Like she was asking him as a friend, not as an employee.

Okay, a friend with maybe some very more-than-friends feelings going on.

He studied her for such a long moment, though, that she worried she shouldn't have asked. The tightening of his jaw she saw probably meant that he was annoyed.

But then he gave a curt nod. "Okay."

"Okay? Really? All right. Um, does right after work sound good? Then I won't have to drive all the way back to Mountain Springs first."

"Right after work is good."

She might have been reading more into his expression than she should, but when he said that, his eyes sparked with something and the corner of his mouth tugged up just the smallest amount. The two together gave her the impression that, regardless of his apparent quest to remain impassive, he was actually happy about going with her.

She smiled all the way back to her desk. She was going to go shopping with Jack. Just the two of them. She pulled out her cards from Gran-gran and leaned the shopping one against her monitor.

And then she wondered for probably the fiftieth time since Monday how it had been for him to walk into her parents' house and see her big, noisy but loving family. What had he thought of it? Had he liked it or wanted to run far from it?

"What happened in there?"

Noelle jerked out of her thoughts at Bridget's question. She'd been lost in her own thoughts so much that she hadn't been paying attention to the fact that there were others around her, and she was apparently broadcasting her feelings all across her face. She needed to stop thinking about Jack at work!

Thankfully, she remembered what she had gone to his office for before she'd gotten distracted with asking him to go shopping. She cleared her throat. "Well, there was no whistling, but I did hear him talking about Christmas shopping, and he didn't sound totally upset about it."

Bridget raised an eyebrow. "I'm impressed. I wonder what made the Grinch change his ways."

Lennox set a stack of papers on Bridget's desk and put a hand up to his mouth and stage-whispered, "Maybe it is a *who*, not a *what*."

Bridget gave Noelle a look of curiosity so strong she was sure she would suggest they investigate. So Noelle gave the most disinterested shrug she could manage while having Jack on the brain and turned back to her work, trying desperately not to show all over her face her hope that maybe it was actually because of her.

Noelle sat on a bench in the main hallway of the mall, glancing down the short hallway that led to the front doors, sipping the last of the cup of wassail she'd gotten from the kiosk next to her. She hadn't planned to get one, but she'd arrived early, and the smells of cinnamon, ginger, nutmeg, and apple cider that had filled the air had just been too much to resist. Even though it was a scent and a taste and a tradition that would forever be inextricably tied to Gran-gran and made a fresh wave of loss wash over her.

She let herself feel the feeling. To let herself miss Gran-gran. But she didn't allow herself to think about her—she wasn't about to start bawling in the middle of the mall, right before her boss met up with her.

She tossed the empty cup into the garbage receptacle just as Jack walked through the front doors. He was still wearing his slacks and light blue button-down, but he'd lost the jacket and tie and had the first couple of buttons unbuttoned. She tried not to stare, but good golly, how had she managed to work with this man for a year and a half without having even a tiny crush? Maybe it was because now that she knew more about who he was and had seen a bit of his heart, he was even more good-looking.

And that smile he gave when his eyes met hers had her knees buckling. It was just a slight one tugging at his lips, but his eyes smiled, too, and it told her that he was glad to see her, even if it was in a mall at Christmastime.

"Hi," she breathed as he neared. Then, realizing how breathy the word had come out, cleared her throat. "Are you ready to tackle this?"

He took a deep breath and looked out at the copious Christmas decorations surrounding them. Towering Christmas trees filled the open area, with giant nutcrackers standing at attention around them. Archways of lights and garlands led into the hallways in all three directions. Reindeer were grazing in fields of puffy cotton snow. Every pillar was wrapped like a giant candy cane, and every kiosk was transformed to look like it belonged at the North Pole.

"I'm pretty sure that if we handled getting the ad campaign for Lelepali Luminaries up and running, we can handle this."

Noelle laughed. That campaign had nearly killed them all before they made it to the end. She didn't think he entirely believed that they'd make it to the end of this, but she'd get him there. "Who do you need to buy for?"

"I've already ordered something for the employees, so just Rachel and Aiden and a couple of friends. And Rachel asked me to pick up some things for her."

"Do you know what you want to get any of them?"

He shook his head. "Rachel gave me her shopping list, but for the gifts I need to get, no."

"Well, I have some ideas for Rachel. There's a store that'll be perfect down this way." As they walked down the giant candy cane- and garland-lined hallways, she couldn't stop thinking about his list. It was such a small group of people to shop for. Her own list was wonderfully, ridiculously, overwhelmingly long. Then she realized something about his list that he hadn't mentioned. "No gifts for parents?"

"No. They passed away."

"Oh." The words felt like a stab. Why had she brought it up when he hadn't mentioned them? "I'm so sorry. I shouldn't have asked."

"It's fine. It was a long time ago. They were in a car together when they got in a terrible crash."

"Was it at Christmastime?" She wondered if that was why he seemed to really dislike the season.

He shook his head. "Summertime." She didn't think he would say anything more—and she definitely wasn't going to ask—but after a long pause, he spoke again. "My parents didn't get along great, so they seldom went places together. But they had gone to an outdoor concert and crashed on the way home. I was fifteen, and Rachel was eighteen. She had just graduated from high school, and the courts allowed her to be my guardian. So for a long time, it was just Rachel and me. Until Aiden came along, of course."

Noelle stopped outside of the store she had been leading them to. "And Aiden's father?"

"He's never been in the picture."

She nodded. She'd guessed that had been the case. As they walked inside, she said, "My Aunt Sharon went through chemotherapy a few years ago. I remember that she was really grateful to have a silk sleep mask that she could use during treatments. Oh, like those over there.

"And if you want to get her some fuzzy socks or a really soft blanket, this would be a good store for that. Maybe even an electric blanket. And there's a great store just a little further down where they have some moisturizers to die for. My aunt had complained about dry skin a lot. And lip balm. Some comfy sweats. Maybe some ginger candies for nausea—I bet we could find some in a candy store or something. Oh! A HEPA air purifier might be good, too." She paused. "What?"

He was giving her a strange look that she couldn't quite interpret. She liked what it did to the corners of his mouth and the brightness of his eyes. Even the slight tilt to his head. But had no idea what it was.

He lifted one shoulder in a shrug but kept those bright eyes on her. "You're really good at this."

She might have blushed. But she hated blushing, so she waved off his comment, commanding her body to do the same, and said, "You haven't seen anything yet. Wait until you witness my ability to find the exact clothing size needed when there doesn't appear to be any. It's legendary."

It wasn't legendary—it just happened sometimes. Why did she say that? She was probably going to get a chance to back up her words with action on this shopping trip, and it was going to be embarrassing when she failed.

He selected a sleep mask and an unbelievably soft electric blanket that would make even the most workaholic insomniac snuggle up and fall right asleep. As they were in line to pay, he said, "Tell me about your grandma. You said she was the most important person to you? And the reason why you took the job to help Aiden?"

All the feelings of loss that she'd been suppressing while being in this mall at Christmastime came rushing back to her at once. She knew she had to get a handle on them quickly or she'd be a sobbing mess. That was very much not how she wanted this shopping trip to go.

She swallowed hard. And then, instead of focusing on how much she missed her right now, she focused on the great memories they had together.

"Gran-gran was ... my person. The one who got me. You met my three older sisters—Becca, Hope, and Julianne—at my parents. They're each just under a year and a half apart in age, but because of when their birthdays fell, they're only a year apart in school. Which meant that they went through a lot of the same milestones very close to the same time. Sports, dance lessons, starting to date, school dances, getting driver's licenses, deciding on a college, and all those kinds of things. They just took a lot of attention, and all three of them needed a lot of it at the same time.

"I am three years younger than them, and Katie is three years younger than me. She got a lot of attention from my parents, too, just by being the youngest. And I was kind of ... forgotten. Not purposely," she quickly added. "My family isn't like that. I just kind of got lost in the middle of it all."

Jack nodded, his face looking thoughtful, but he stayed quiet, waiting for her to continue. But then it was their turn at the register, so she held off on her story until the items were paid for, in a bag, and they were heading out of that shop and onto the next one.

"Gran-gran was a middle child, too, and she knew entirely too well what that felt like. She always made me feel not forgotten. Important. But not only that, we just got along really well. Like from the moment I was born. She always used to say that we'd been best friends in heaven and that I sure took my sweet time coming to earth so she could get her BFF back."

Jack chuckled. It was a good sound. And it made her realize how good it was for her to talk about all of this. As much as she thought that doing things like this that she used to only do with Gran-gran would be painful, doing them with Jack was actually helping her heart. Like it was nourishing it and allowing it to heal.

"She loved Christmas more than anything, so of course, I did, too. And we did a lot of Christmas traditions together. The cards I got from her were the things we used to do together, painted by her. I still have no idea how they showed up on my doorstep, but I know that she wanted me to continue doing them."

"Well," Jack said, giving a nod to what they were doing together, "I am very grateful that your gran-gran sent them to you." The look on his face was sweet and playful but also had something more, hiding just below the surface. A longing, maybe?

Whatever it was, it was beautiful and made her stomach flutter.

CHAPTER EIGHT

Jack

"So, these cards that your gran-gran sent you. Was shopping on one of them?"

She glanced at him as she led him toward a toy store. "It was."

He shouldn't ask. But hearing more about these cards helped him know her better, and he desperately wanted to know her better. It was a need that he knew was dangerous, but they were here, and she seemed to really enjoy talking about her gran-gran. So he wanted her to keep talking, knowing full well that the more he got to know her, the harder it would be for him to be around her and not pursue a relationship.

"What were your traditions around that? Because if your gran-gran wanted you to do that, maybe we should."

He was expecting a quick response, so when it didn't come, he glanced over at her. She seemed hesitant. He didn't know if it was painful or because she didn't want to do it with him. Maybe she needed to do it with her own family. He shouldn't have asked.

But then she said, "Are you sure?" like she didn't think he would want to.

"Of course."

He shouldn't have worked so hard to talk her into doing any Christmas activities with Aiden. He had his own issues with Christmas, so he should've respected that she had hers. He probably wouldn't have pushed if he hadn't already been so drawn to her. But he'd been drawn to her for so long and had kept it all in check for a year and a half. Why could he not seem to now?

They stepped just inside Taheny's Toys, and she picked up a bucket of slime that was big enough that it took both hands. And that was when he noticed that her cheeks were a bit pink. Was she embarrassed?

"Do you promise not to laugh?"

So she *was* embarrassed. He nodded, a smile already tugging at his lips.

"As we shopped, we wrote bad ad copy hooks for the items we saw."

His eyebrows rose, and a chuckle of disbelief escaped his mouth before he could stop it. "As a kid, you did this?"

"Yep. The dorkier the ad copy, the better. Gran-gran had a job in marketing, and writing bad ad copy made me want to become a copywriter. Growing up, no one else my age even knew what ad copy was or what the job of a copywriter entailed, so it was kind of a special thing only between Gran-gran and me."

"Huh. So that's why you're so good at it."

She turned the bucket of slime around in her hands. "Are you saying that writing bad ad copy made me good at my job?"

"Don't tell me it didn't help you recognize good ad copy." He nodded at the slime. "What would you write for that?"

She studied it for a moment, then, in a voice he could only describe as an announcer's, said, "It's ooey. It's gooey. It's stretchy. It's slimy. And if you get this for your kid this Christmas, then by New Year's you'll know just how many objects in your house a three-pound bucket can stretch to cover."

He laughed, and they went into the store and started walking down the aisles. They made their way through the store, getting the things Rachel had asked him to pick up. He also found a few toys that he wanted to give to Aiden and got those, too.

All along the way, one of them would pick up a toy and say some bad ad copy in the same announcer voice that Noelle had first used. He held up a bin of Legos and said, "We could target parents and say, 'Want to level-up your ability to find sharp pieces while barefooted in the dark? Get the one thousand piece set for your overly-enthusiastic child.'"

Noelle found a stuffed elf that looked more like he belonged in a horror movie than on a shelf. "Think you've been getting too much sleep lately? Put this creepy toy in your kid's room, and you'll never have that problem again."

He laughed and pointed out an electronic drum set that was on display and fully worked, much to the thrill of all the kids in the store. "Did your brother buy your kid a xylophone last Christmas? Buy his kid these drums. It's the ultimate one-up he'll never be able to top."

"Oh, and then we could do an ad with all the noisy toys on it, and the ad copy could say, 'Think you might want noise-canceling headphones for Christmas? Trust us: you do.'"

He was pretty sure he had never had as much fun in a toy store before, not even as a kid. He definitely knew it was worlds above every other Christmas shopping experience he'd ever had.

She picked up a toy doll. "Do you want kids?"

"I like Aiden. I wouldn't mind having some kids for myself sometime. I just haven't found 'the one' yet." Not that he'd been looking. But he was suddenly curious about her. "You?"

"Of course. I just haven't found 'the one,' either."

He picked up a box containing a race car track but didn't really look at it at all. He needed to prod. To find out more. And the only way he could think to do that was to offer more himself. "I've just always kind of assumed that marriage isn't for me. I never looked at my parents' marriage and thought, 'I want that for me someday.' Not that I'm against marriage—I know there are plenty of good marriages out there. I guess I've just never had a lot of faith that it'd happen for me." His issues weren't deep, but they were still there a bit.

She was silent for a moment. Maybe taking in what he'd just said, or perhaps trying to decide if she wanted to share anything. He hoped she did. "Have you ever gotten to the point of talking about marriage with anyone you dated?" Okay, that was really pushing for personal information. He couldn't believe he'd asked it.

She shook her head. "Not really. A few had gotten a little more serious, but I think I knew long before we broke up that it wasn't heading toward marriage. I do look at my parents and think, 'I want that for me.' I just haven't found my person. The one who will look at me the way my dad looks at my mom."

Was it wrong that he suddenly desperately wanted to be that person for her? Yes. It very much was. He forced himself to break eye contact with her and set down the box. "We should probably go pay."

She nodded. He didn't know what was going through her head just then, but he could tell that it was a lot. He needed to lighten things up a bit.

As they walked out of the store, arms laden with bags, they got away from the noise enough to hear the Christmas music filling the halls. He never listened to Christmas music by choice, but he still knew the song right away—*The First Noel*. "Oh, hey, it's your song."

"I love this song! When I was little and would see 'noel' everywhere at this time of year, I would always tell anyone who would listen that they spelled it wrong."

Jack chuckled. "Did it ever bother you to have a name that was linked to a holiday season?"

"No, because I was born on Christmas Eve. My birthday is super entwined with Christmas, so it feels right that my name would be, too."

"I'm guessing that having a Christmas Eve birthday didn't help with feeling forgotten."

Noelle laughed a big hearty laugh that people didn't do in public nearly often enough. It made him smile. "No. But it has its perks, too. One year, when I was probably five, my dad had just finished reading us the poem *The Night Before Christmas*. At the end, he said the words, 'Happy Christmas to all, and to all a goodnight!' and Becca shouted, 'Happy birthday to Noelle,' and like they planned it, but they hadn't, everyone else shouted, 'And to Noelle a good night!'

"Every year since, as my family gets together for Christmas Eve, someone will randomly shout out 'Happy birthday to Noelle,' and everyone else will stop what they're doing and shout back 'And to Noelle a good night!' My nieces and nephews especially like it."

"That's actually pretty sweet."

"Yeah. What about your name? Does it come with anything significant?"

He shrugged. "I was born in January. A frigid January, as the story goes. My dad wanted to name me Jack Frost because he thought it would be funny. I'm not really sure you should choose a baby's name based on what you think is funny, but that's my dad for you. Thankfully, my mom wouldn't let him. Their compromise was to name me Jack with the middle initial F."

"If it helps, my parents didn't give me a middle name, so my full name is Noelle Allred. Whenever I have to sign my initials, I have to put 'NA.' Like I'm writing that it's just not applicable to me."

He laughed. "Weirdly, that does help. My last name helps, too. Meadows is a word with very springtime connotations, so it kind of undermined my dad's plan. I never knew if he wanted to name me Jack Frost in hopes that I would be the sprightly character of myths or if he named me that because he thought I was the Bringer of Cold. On days when he was sober, I liked to think it was because of the sprightly character. On days when he was drinking and was an ornery cuss—which was most of the time during the holidays—I was sure it was the Bringer of Cold."

"Is that why you don't like Christmas?"

He had told her the story to be funny but hadn't thought about how much it would bring out the negative parts. "Yeah. Every Christmassy thing that my mom tried to have us do, my dad always turned into a big blowup. So everything Christmas-related is very tied to memories of my dad being at his worst and making all of us miserable."

She was quiet for a long moment, and he was sure he was going to get pity from her, which he very much did not want. He also really didn't want to talk about it anymore.

Instead, she asked, "Have you ever heard of exposure therapy?"

"You expose yourself to your greatest fear to get over it, right?"

"Right. So, I had a deathly fear of heights. If it was because of some traumatic childhood experience, I know nothing about it. But it was there regardless. When I was in high school, I got a job at a ski resort in Nestled Hollow. I thought I'd just be making hot chocolate in the lodge, seeing cute guys, stuff like that."

"I think I can see where this is headed."

"Yep. For an entire snow season, I was assigned to be the lift operator up the mountain. Every single day I had to ride the tram to the top, and I was terrified—pulse racing, heart pumping, hyperventilating, all of it. I was so convinced I was going to die. But by the end of the season, not only was I still alive, but I wasn't afraid of heights anymore. I think it has something to do with the emotions tied to the event. So instead of terrified feelings being tied to heights, it turned to safe feelings being tied to it, since I was safe every single time."

"And you think I should do that with Christmas?"

Noelle shrugged. "Well, right now you've got some pretty negative feelings tied to it, so you hate it. But if you were around Christmassy things a lot and had positive feelings tied to it, those feelings would overtake the negative ones." Then she said, almost in a whisper, "Maybe we both need that."

He looked at her for a long time, not quite knowing how to respond.

She must've switched from thinking about how much she needed it to thinking about how much he did because the next time she spoke, her voice wasn't a whisper at all. It was full of confidence. "When I took the side job to help provide Aiden with Christmas experiences, I told you that you needed to come to half of the activities. I think you should come to all of them."

He met her eyes. Could he commit to that? He was probably at the halfway mark of attending Christmas events right now and could easily bow out of the rest of them. If he agreed, then not only would he be facing more of a holiday he'd hated for his entire life, but he'd be spending a lot more time around Noelle.

The exposure therapy for Christmas might just work to turn it into a holiday he loved. But exposure to more of Noelle might just make him fall more in love with her, too. And he knew just how dangerous that would be to his heart.

But still, he found himself nodding and saying, "Okay, it's a deal."

CHAPTER NINE

Noelle

Noelle pulled up in front of her parents' house in her own car. It was so nice to have Elfie back! It wasn't as nice as the rental she'd been driving, but it was great to feel "home" again in her car. She opened the back door to let Aiden and his dog, Bailey, out. Aiden immediately grabbed Bailey's leash and ran across the lawn, weaving between all the lawn decorations, to where her family was congregating around the hot chocolate before the hayride, excited to introduce his dog to her parents' dog, Captain.

Noelle went around to help Rachel out of the car, but she was doing well enough that she was out before Noelle even got there. She looped her arm in Rachel's like they were sisters, so she was right there if Rachel needed any help.

They walked through the mostly tramped-down snow, around the nativity and the giant ornaments. Rachel looked to where Aiden was making himself at home with Noelle's family. "Thank you so much for all you've done for Aiden. You've gone well beyond everything I was hoping for him."

Noelle looked at Aiden, too. "He's a cool kid. I've enjoyed every moment of it. And I'm so glad you're feeling well enough to join us for the hayride! It's one of my favorite traditions, and if you're going to experience one, this is it. It was my gran-gran's favorite, too."

Rachel smiled as they made their way across the snow-covered ground. "From what little I've heard of your gran-gran, she sounds like she was a pretty cool person."

"She was. I was kind of worried about today because it was one of our favorite traditions, but I'm doing better than I thought I would. Last year, celebrating felt like we were just ignoring that she was no longer with us. This year, though, it feels like we are honoring her by continuing the traditions she loved."

"It sounds like that's what she would've wanted." Rachel smiled and gave her arm a little squeeze. "Thank you for including me."

Based on the Christmas decorations in Rachel's yard, Noelle figured that she actually did like the holiday. She probably hadn't been able to celebrate it much at all, though. "Do you think it might make you nauseous? We do go pretty slow, but it's sometimes a little bumpy."

"I'm doing pretty good today, actually. I think I'll be okay."

Noelle grinned and led them toward the table filled with hot chocolate supplies where all of her family was congregating.

This year, she was even more excited about the hayride. Not only was Jack coming, but Rachel was there, too. Which meant that she'd be able to get some more info about Jack.Now that she was seeing his personal side and finding out more and more about him, the more she wanted to know. She felt like she was stranded in the desert, and information about Jack was a jug of cool water—she just couldn't get enough of it.

It didn't take long after Noelle introduced Rachel to her parents and sisters and their spouses and kids that Rachel was chatting with her and her sisters like they had known each other their whole lives. And it didn't take long for Noelle to start picturing her as a sister-in-law.

Stop that, she chided herself. *Nothing is happening between you and your boss, so stop setting yourself up for heartbreak.*

And then Jack pulled up in front of her parents' house and got out of his car. When his eyes found hers, he wore an expression that had her whispering out loud, "Or maybe I'm wrong." Because the smile on his face felt like it was just for her. It quirked up on one side just slightly more than the other, and his eyes were all soft and warm, and it made her stomach flutter and happiness wash over her. And gosh, he looked good even in a wool coat, gloves, a hat, and a scarf.

His eyes stayed on her as he walked around the lawn decorations and across the snow, only leaving hers for a moment while he went up to Rachel, gave her a hug, then gave a nod toward the hot chocolate. She nodded, then his eyes were immediately back on Noelle's. So, of course, she took a couple of steps to the hot chocolate table.

"Hi," he said, and it felt like so much was loaded into that single word.

"Hi," she breathed back, practically melting. Then, realizing that her dad was at the hot chocolate table, ladle in hand, she cleared her throat and said, "Would you like some hot chocolate?"

Jack nodded. "I'll get some for Rachel first."

Aiden noticed that his uncle had arrived, so he came running over from where he'd been playing with his new friends, Bailey at his side. Her dad ladled up hot chocolate into four cups, and Noelle helped Aiden make his—mixing in chocolate chips and a massive scoop of whipped cream—while Jack added caramel and a pinch of sea salt to Rachel's.

Then she and Jack started making their own. She reached for the spoon in the raspberry jelly, her favorite hot chocolate mix-in, at the same time as Jack reached for it, their hands bumping. "You like raspberry in yours?" No one in her family liked it. Well, except for Gran-gran.

He looked at her, surprise on his face. "You do, too?"

The biggest shock, though, was when they both reached for the cayenne pepper next.

"No way," Noelle's dad said. "I thought Noelle was the only person on the planet who liked raspberry and cayenne in hot chocolate."

Jack gave her that smile she loved that quirked up more on one side. "I've always thought she had impeccable taste."

"Corbin," Katie said to Becca's husband as she pulled her phone out of her pocket. "Are you ready for an interview?"

As the two of them headed away from the crowd and the kids running underfoot for a bit, Noelle and Jack took Rachel's hot chocolate to her.

Her mom came over at the same time and said, "Rachel, we're so glad to have you here! And if you're feeling up to it and don't have other plans, you should join us for Christmas Eve dinner. It's Noelle's birthday, too, so we always have a big celebration. We would love to have you."

Rachel looked like she was touched to be invited and said she would attend if it was at all possible, and it looked like she really meant it. Jack looked happy to be asked, too. This might end up being her favorite birthday / Christmas Eve ever.

Her mom motioned to the truck that had two flatbed trailers connected to it like a train. Both had hay bales arranged in a rectangle, with bales stacked two high in the middle for backrests so that people could sit on all four sides on each trailer. They had already laid blankets across all of them so they wouldn't be itchy. "I want to make sure you're in the spot that's going to be most comfortable. I know that chemo can make you really nauseous; which spot do you think will be best for keeping that at bay?"

"Oh, um, probably facing the direction we are driving. Maybe on the second trailer?"

Her mom winked. "I'll get it ready for you."

Then they all headed toward the trailers and found seats. Noelle's mom had put extra padding in the spot where Rachel would be sitting, and her dad told all the little kids they couldn't jump around on that trailer. Rachel seemed to love having Noelle's parents fawn over her. She glanced at Jack. He was watching Rachel, too, seeming to love seeing her love it.

"Okay, how this works," Noelle said as she leaned over Jack, who was sitting by Rachel, "is that we drive around and look at all the lights. But every once in a while, we'll stop at a house, jump off the trailer, then all go up to sing Christmas carols."

Then her mom turned on the Christmas music and her dad, who was sitting in the driver's seat of the truck, pulled it gently away from the curb. They started heading down the street, the chill in the slight wind causing all of them to pull their hats on a little tighter and to reach for the extra blankets piled on the top of the middle hay bales. Jack stood up and grabbed one of the blankets and placed it over Rachel and Aiden, tucking it in at their sides. Then he grabbed a second one, sat down, and wrapped it around himself and Noelle.

Was it wrong to snuggle into him? Because it was so cold, and he was so warm, and the blanket was kind of pulling them together a bit. Plus, he smelled divine. She took in another deep breath just to smell the sweet pine scent again, even though the cold burned her nose.

His hand was on his leg, but his pinky rested up against her thigh. As they drove past all the beautiful lights people had used to decorate their houses and yards, his finger moved, hesitantly at first, brushing so slightly against her jeans, sending thrills up her spine. It was the slightest touch, but it felt monumental.

She hesitated a very long moment, then decided to just take a gamble and reached for his hand. She heard him suck in a breath like she had surprised him, but then he entwined his fingers in hers as the music played and the lights sparkled, and a light snow drifted down from the sky.

"Hey, Aiden," Katie said as she took a seat next to him and Bailey. "Are you going to dress this cute dog of yours up for the pet costume parade?"

Aiden looked to Noelle. So she nodded and said, "You bet we are. My gran-gran and I used to dress up her dog Daisy every year—it's so much fun."

He grinned and turned back to Katie, so she said, "Can I interview you for the video I'm putting together to watch on Christmas Eve?"

"Yes!" Aiden said, pumping a fist. "I was hoping I'd get to be in it!"

With her phone aimed at Aiden, Katie said, "What's your favorite part about Christmas?"

"Being with my mom." He paused for a moment, then he added, "And making decorations, like the snowflakes that are hanging from our ceiling. And doing all of the activities with Uncle Jack and Noelle."

"You're new to this hayride," Katie said. "Tell us about how you're joining us this year, so when we watch this when we're old and gray, we'll remember why."

"Well," Aiden said, settling against the hay bale at his back, his voice ringing out loud and clear, "I heard my mom telling Uncle Jack that she wanted me to do fun Christmas things, and he got Noelle to help. At first, my mom wasn't all the way happy about that, but only because we hadn't met Noelle yet.

"*But* Mrs. Sowards brought us over a meal one night. They thought I was in my room, but I was actually sitting under the kitchen table. And I heard Mom tell Mrs. Sowards that she was glad that Jack asked Noelle for help because Jack has been more smiley since he started hanging out with Noelle.

"And," Aiden said in a whisper loud enough that everyone on both trailers heard—and probably her dad, too, since he had his window rolled down, "she thinks he's pretty much in love with her. You know, the kind of love where there's kissing and marriage and sneaking food off each other's plates."

Noelle felt Jack stiffen.

Rachel gasped. "Aiden!"

"What? I whispered it, so they didn't hear."

Then Rachel turned to her and Jack. "I am so sorry. And I didn't say anything about the kissing and plates and marriage thing. That was all him."

There was an uncomfortable, awkward silence. But also, it came with a feeling of hope.

Her dad must've either heard Aiden or sensed the tension because he pulled over to the side of the road, giving everyone something else to think about.

"Hop off for a caroling stop!" her mom called out, and everyone threw off their blankets and got off of the trailer, the two dogs included.

"Are you coming?" Noelle asked Jack.

He shook his head. "I need to stay here and help my sister."

Rachel didn't look like she needed help, but if she had been Jack, she would've stayed behind, too. She got off the trailer and grabbed hold of the hand Aiden wasn't using to hold Bailey's leash and walked with everyone else up to the porch of their neighbor's house.

She took one glance back at the trailers as Hope knocked on the door and saw Jack straightening Rachel's blanket and making sure it was tucked in around her so the cold couldn't get in. It was so sweet that he was so protective of her.

After a rousing rendition of "Silent Night," where the dogs joined in and did their best to sing, too, they headed back to the trailer. This time, Jack didn't sit close enough that their legs touched. He didn't reach out with a pinky to brush her leg, and he didn't take her hand in his. She felt the loss keenly. That hope Aiden had given her felt a little less potent.

As they turned down another road, Rachel said, "Hey, my friend Amy lives in that house up there on the left. She has brought me so many meals while I've been going through chemo."

Noelle's mom, who was riding in the closer trailer, called out to her dad, "Stop at that blue house on the left."

Before Jack got any other ideas, Noelle said, "I'll stay with Rachel this time—it's your turn to go up and sing."

He shook his head. "I don't—"

But Rachel interrupted with, "Will you tell Amy I said hi?"

Noelle was close enough to see the muscle in his jaw working, but then he gave a nod and called out to where Aiden was now sitting with Noelle's nephews. "Come on, buddy. Let's go sing."

Aiden and Bailey both leaped off the trailer and ran around to take Jack's hand before walking up to the home. Noelle watched them, impressed that Jack was willing to go, even though he had such bad associations with Christmas, he didn't sing, and he probably didn't know Christmas songs very well.

"What's Jack like at work?"

Noelle scooted closer to Rachel so they could talk more easily. "Very professional and closed off. He doesn't get personal, ever."

Rachel laughed. "I wondered if that was what he was like since he always seems so concerned about professionalism. Well, that and the fact that he always goes to work dressed in a suit. But outside of work, he's sweet. Thoughtful. Fun."

She had seen a lot of that over the last couple of weeks. It was a side of him she was growing to love. "What was he like as a kid?"

Rachel looked up like she was thinking about where to start. Then she said, "When our parents died, he hit a bit of a rebellious stage. Which I totally understood—it was such a hard time. I was eighteen, and suddenly I was his guardian, and I had no idea how to be the mom of a fifteen-year-old. I had mothered him a lot all of his life, but this was different.

"And it wasn't that he was rebelling against me—it was more that he was mad at the world because so many things had been stacked against us. He just stayed out past curfew, got some questionable friends, started dressing differently, things like that. I knew it was likely just part of the grief process and how he dealt with it. But I was so worried for him and didn't know how best to help.

"After a few months, there was a night when he'd left with friends and hadn't been in the best headspace. Before, he'd missed curfew by an hour or two. That night, it was four hours past, and I worried myself sick every single second of those four hours. By the time he got home, I was a complete wreck.

"He came home and saw exactly what that night had done to me. I swear, he stopped being rebellious right then." She snapped her fingers. "Like flipping a switch. He somehow figured things out and pulled himself out of it. I think he realized that he was piling even more stress on me when things had already been hard enough for both of us.

"But he'd always been a sweet, thoughtful kid. When we were little, our dad would drink a lot and get verbally abusive. Just mean. Sometimes physically mean. We learned to just stay away whenever he was drinking. Our mom dealt with it by closing herself off and shutting down, so Jack and I had to rely on each other a lot. Since I was the big sister, I acted like the mom when our mom wasn't.

"When we were small and putting ourselves to bed, he *always* thanked me for taking care of him. I've never known anyone to be as grateful as he is. One night, after he thanked me, he said, 'But there's no one taking care of you.' There wasn't. And I really felt it, you know? I nearly started bawling right then and there just to have it acknowledged.

"So from that night on, he always told *me* a bedtime story, so I'd be taken care of, too. He made up his own before he was old enough to read and did a mix of reading stories to me and making up stories as he got older. I swear that was what made me survive our childhood. I'm lucky to have him as a brother."

Noelle's eyes were misting at hearing how his childhood was and how sweet he was through it. She looked over at where he stood at Amy's porch, holding Bailey's leash in one hand and holding Aiden, who was perched on his shoulder, with the other hand.

"He's going to make a really good dad someday."

Rachel nodded. "The best."

Noelle tried not to imagine him being a dad to their own kids. She knew how dangerous that kind of thinking was.

Yet, a part of her still imagined it anyway. And it must've been showing on her face because when Jack and everyone else came back to the trailers, he was giving her a curious look like he was trying to interpret her expression.

And this time when he sat down, he pulled the blanket around them snugly, so she cozied right into him.

When they made it through all the lights in town and back to her parents' house, everyone started saying their goodbyes. Jack had planned to take both Rachel and Aiden home, but Aiden said, "Can I *please* ride back with Noelle? She has windows that you roll down by turning a handle instead of pushing a button!"

Okay, her little Kia Rio was not that old—it just happened to have manual windows. Hearing Aiden talk about it made it sound like it was several decades old.

“It’s freezing out here, buddy,” Jack said, his hands deep in his pockets, shivering a bit as he said it. “You shouldn’t be rolling the windows down.”

“I only roll them down when we’re at a stoplight, so no wind blows in. Noelle said it was okay. Please?” he said, dragging out the word to the full extent his lungs could manage.

Rachel and Jack both looked at Noelle as if asking for permission. So she smiled at the adorable kid. “Sure thing, kiddo.”

True to his word, he only rolled down the window when they were stopped. But it was at every stop sign and stoplight on the way home. At least they were already used to the cold temperatures.

After getting Aiden and Rachel inside their home and saying their goodbyes, Jack walked her out to her trusty car.

He leaned against Elfie, which made her smile. It meant that he wasn’t planning to leave super quickly, and she was in no way ready for him to go. “Thanks for making me come tonight. I actually rather enjoyed it.”

She grinned and stepped a little closer to him. She didn’t lean against the car—that thing was freezing cold—but she got within a foot of Jack’s warmth. “Are those negative feelings about Christmas changing yet?”

This time, he reached out for her hand. And, even though they were wearing gloves, the feel of his hand in hers still sent shivers of happiness up her. “They are. I think they started changing before I even noticed it.”

His voice was low and gruff, yet with the perfect amount of smoothness, too. It was mesmerizing, and she just wanted him to talk to her with that voice all night long. It didn't even matter what he said—it could be his to-do list for tomorrow, and she'd still be enthralled.

He gave her hand the slightest tug. An invitation to come closer if she wanted to, but still slight enough that she could pretend she didn't notice. But it wasn't like she was going to ignore it. She stepped even closer, her leg pressing against his. "I am more than happy to keep helping with that exposure therapy. You're coming to the Santa Mystery Hat thing tomorrow, right?" They were so close that her words came out as a whispered breath in the crisp night air, the words making little puffs of warmth in the cold night air.

"Of course," he breathed, his lips just inches from hers.

Her eyes searched his, trying to unravel everything he might be thinking, and his eyes searched right back, probably trying to guess what she was thinking, too. She could search his eyes all night long and not tire of it.

And then a car drove past, and whatever spell they had been under was broken in an instant. Jack stood up straight and said, "We shouldn't. I'm your boss."

"Yeah," she said, acknowledging the part about him being her boss, wishing it hadn't sounded like she was also acknowledging the "we shouldn't" part.

He gave her hand a squeeze, then said, "I'll see you tomorrow night?"

She nodded as he opened Elfie's door, then she gave him a smile as she sat in her seat. At least they had tomorrow.

CHAPTER TEN

Jack

The entire day, Jack had been thinking about how he'd almost kissed Noelle last night. A part of him wished they had kissed—he so wanted to. He had wanted to for the past couple of weeks. For the last year and a half, actually.

But a more significant part of him was terrified that he'd come so close to very nearly kissing her. She was his employee. He was her boss. Kissing Noelle wasn't on the table.

Since it was a Saturday and he wasn't hurrying to get off work, he told Noelle that he would pick Aiden up for the Santa Hat thing because he wanted to check on Rachel. When he walked into their house, though, Aiden didn't come running to leap onto him to give him a hug.

Rachel poked her head out from the back of the house and held a finger to her lips, motioning for him to be quiet. As he got closer, she whispered, "Between the hayride last night and sledding this afternoon with Quinton's family, he was tuckered out. We just ate, and he fell asleep at the table just a few minutes ago. I'm sorry I didn't realize how tired he was before you drove all the way here."

"It's no problem." He walked into the kitchen and saw his little nephew slumped back into his chair, soundly asleep. He was glad he came; he would've hated for Rachel to have had to try to carry him into his room. She might have been doing better the past few days, but something like that would've been too much.

He scooped Aiden into his arms and carried him to his room, placing him on his bed and pulling the covers up to his shoulders. Then he gave his hair a ruffle and stepped out of his room, carefully pulling the door closed behind him.

He was surprised at how disappointed he was that they wouldn't be going to the activity with Noelle's family. He was actually starting to really like those celebrations so much more than he thought he ever could.

He looked around Rachel's kitchen and family room area. "Since I'm here, what do you need help with? I can clean or do dishes..."

Rachel shook her head. "No. I'm pretty tuckered. Since Aiden is asleep this early, I'd like the chance to go to sleep this early, too." She paused. "But you should still go to the activity."

He should. He told Noelle he would be there, and he didn't want to let her down. And he had agreed to the exposure therapy thing. But they had also very nearly kissed last night. He had been so successful at keeping things professional with her for so long, and last night, he came so close to completely failing. Could he even trust himself to be with her more?

"You told her you would go," Rachel said in a stern voice. "You should keep your word."

Rachel knew him well enough to know exactly what to say to get him to go. He really didn't want to go back on his word. The part of him that had wished he had just kissed her last night celebrated.

The other part was going to have to be on high alert.

When he arrived at Noelle's parents' house, Noelle seemed genuinely sad that Aiden couldn't come. The two of them appeared to have bonded more strongly than he would've guessed.

"Okay," Noelle's dad said, holding a Santa hat by the white fur trim and shaking its contents, "we've got six teams and six papers inside. Two for the dinner, two for the entertainment, and two for the decorations. Are you all ready for this?"

Everyone cheered, and Jack looked around. Noelle and her four sisters were each standing with their spouses—a date for Katie—and had their kids with them. It seemed that each sister was a team with her own family, so the sixth team must be her parents and Captain, who was sitting upright at their feet, clearly thinking he was on the team to beat. Jack was glad he hadn't skipped coming—it would've left Noelle in a team by herself.

Noelle rubbed her hands together, eyes on the Santa hat, seeming full of anticipation at what they would draw out. It made him smile. Her dad took the hat to Hope, and she drew out a paper and then said out loud, "Dinner."

"Let's hope that Katie doesn't get the other 'Dinner' paper," Noelle said, apparently kicking off the smack-talk portion of the evening.

"Hey, I heard that," Katie said. Then, after a pause, she added, "But really, even I'm hoping for that."

Noelle leaned in close to him, and he tried to ignore the way it kicked his heart rate up a notch. "If we get dinner, we have thirty minutes from the time we leave the house to the time we get back to shop for food. We'll have twenty dollars, and we'll have to buy ingredients that the *other* team will use to make a meal. The challenge is to buy things that in no way will go together. We'd have thirty minutes to cook once we get back."

His eyebrows rose. "Let's hope we don't get that one, then."

Her dad took the hat to Becca next, and she drew out one and said, "Entertainment!" and her three older kids pumped their fists.

He leaned in and whispered, "What's that one?"

She kept her eyes on the Santa hat but whispered, "Each team will have fifteen minutes to gather props and costumes from anywhere in the house. Then they give what they collected to the other team. Then each team has forty-five minutes to come up with a skit using those props and costumes and practice it."

Wow. Her family really did the high-pressure activities here. He felt completely out of his league.

Then her dad brought the hat to Noelle, and she drew out a paper. "Yes! We got decorations!"

She was so excited that it made him smile.

She leaned in and said, "Okay, they'll have a list of things we need to get, and we'll have forty-five minutes to get them. Then, when we get back, we'll have fifteen minutes to decorate a small tree with what we collected."

That didn't seem too hard. He could do this.

Katie and her date drew out the other "Skit" paper; Julianne, her husband, and her two kids were going to decorate the second tree; and Noelle's parents drew the other "Dinner" paper.

"Okay," her mom called out, "you've got five minutes to huddle and come up with a game plan. When you hear the horn, your timer for the games starts!"

Noelle grabbed one of the papers her dad held out, then grabbed Jack's hand and pulled him into the living room that was right next to the front door as the rest of the family scattered to different locations. A tree that was probably two and a half or three feet high and already had lights on it sat on a table in the middle of the room.

She put her hand on it. "Our challenge is basically a scavenger hunt for items to decorate this tree. We have to get something that fits each of the items on this list.

The more creative, the better, since everyone votes on which team wins."

"What's at stake?"

"Bragging rights and a trophy. Whoever wins it keeps it for a year and proudly displays it. The next year, they have to give it up to whoever won that category. And Jack? We really want to win."

He smiled, loving this competitive side of her. He glanced at the list of five items. "We can probably go to that craft store on Main Street and get all of this."

She shook her head. "We can't get more than one thing at any one place, and we can't spend more than ten dollars total. So it has to mostly be things that are free or that we can ask someone for." She gestured to a little table. "We have a hot glue gun, scissors, tape, markers, um, it looks like a couple of hole punches—one a circle and one a square—but we don't have time to get too crafty. We need to keep it simple. And come up with a theme."

Okay, maybe they didn't get the easy one. He was *definitely* out of his league.

Noelle tapped a finger on the list. "Something edible... What kind of food would make a good decoration? Gumdrops are too small... Oh! I saw holiday pretzels at the convenience store just right out on Center. They were shaped like stars. Maybe we can do a theme around that."

Jack nodded. Okay, some direction. He had no idea what to do with the direction, but it sounded good.

"Something sparkly or shiny... Hmm. And something red or blue. That one's easy enough—we could always get a roll of ribbon at the craft store to glue to the back of the pretzels to hang them with. Then we need something found outside and some kind of garland."

Yep. Totally out of his depth.

And then an idea hit. "Something outside—I saw a giant pine tree two houses up. I bet there are pine cones under it still. Maybe we could get some for decorations or...Oh. Maybe if we get five"—he grabbed the markers and laid them out on the table like he was making a big asterisk—"we could put them like this and glue the inside right here to make a star."

"That's genius!" Noelle said, grabbing his arm and making him feel pretty proud of himself for thinking of it.

"Now we just need something sparkly or shiny and some kind of garland. What goes with stars? We can't just have the entire tree be stars. Planets? No. Moons? No." She shook her hands out. "I can't think of anything that goes with stars. What else is in the sky?"

As soon as she said that, all he could think of was helping Aiden to hang all the snowflakes he'd made from the ceiling of their family room. "How about 'Snow under the Stars' for the theme? Maybe we can cut out snowflakes."

"Ooo," she said. "I like that. Okay, we need something sparkly or shiny. I know that the craft store has sheets of paper that are a shiny silver. Maybe we can make the snowflakes out of that. It's thicker paper, so we won't be able to be too intricate with them, but I think we can make it work."

"That's two things from the craft store, though."

"Sixty seconds!" Noelle's mom called out from somewhere else in the house.

"Eek! You're right. We've got to move fast. Um... Oh! The woman who lives on the corner makes handmade cards. She's bound to have ribbon—let's ask her. What are we going to do for a garland?"

"Maybe something with the snow theme? Like tissues or something?" It sounded stupid, but it was the only idea he had.

"Oh! Tissue paper. We could get white—it's everywhere and super cheap. There's an antique store next to the craft store, and they use it to wrap up breakable trinkets. We could try there. We could cut the sheets like big snowflakes and then, I don't know, tape them together into a long garland and then bunch it with ribbon."

A loud horn sounded.

"Huddle time is up!" Noelle's mom called out. "You have sixty minutes from right now to be back here to present what your team has come up with!"

Noelle grinned at him, her eyes lit with excitement. It was coming so strongly off her that he was feeling it himself. "Are you ready?"

He nodded and grinned back. They both slipped on their coats, then she grabbed his hand and pulled him outside. They raced to the neighbor with the pine tree first, knocked on the door, got permission to take "as many pinecones as you'd like—feel free to take them all!" and grabbed seven, just in case. Then they ran just as quickly to the house on the corner.

A woman who was probably in her seventies answered the door, and when Noelle explained what they were doing, she said, "Of course, dear! Come into my craft room. No, don't take off your shoes—you've got a race to win!"

In less than two minutes, they had a roll of ice blue ribbon in their hands, and they were racing back to where his car was parked. He dumped the pine cones onto the floor behind his seat, then they got into the car, and he headed toward the convenience store.

Luckily, they had the pretzels in stock. Noelle picked up two big bags of them and put them on the counter.

Jack's eyebrows drew together. "Why two?"

"Because Aiden is going to wake up tomorrow morning and realize he slept right through this activity, and he's going to feel bad. I figured I could take a bag over to him tomorrow and hang out with him for a bit so he won't feel like he missed so much."

Jack just stared at Noelle. They were in the middle of a race against the clock, trying to win a prize that seemed really important to her, and she was stopping to think of someone who was vastly important to him? It touched him in a way that left him speechless.

She put her credit card back in her pocket, grabbed the bag from the cashier, and said, "Come on!" and they both raced out of the store.

When they were in the car and driving toward the craft store, he asked, "So who would you be on a team with if Aiden and I weren't coming this year?" He came so close to not attending this once he found out that Aiden wasn't.

She was quiet for a long moment before she answered. Then she cleared her throat and said, "I don't know. But it kind of requires six teams. This event has evolved over the years—before everyone started getting married and having kids, we used to do it with cousins, aunts, and uncles. Their families have grown, too, so they do their own versions of it now. For as long as I can remember, Gran-gran had always been my teammate. We didn't do it last year since we were planning a funeral, so this was the first year without her."

He felt an acute pain from what had almost happened. What if he'd just stayed at Rachel's and helped out around her house and not come at all? He felt sick just thinking of how it would be for her to face this first event without her gran-gran and have to do it without a teammate.

He could feel the emotions coming from her as she, too, likely thought about what the night would've been like if he hadn't come. Maybe if he and Aiden had never planned to come, she would've asked one of her cousins or a friend to join her. He was glad it was him here, though.

"What was your favorite time when you pulled *Decorations* from Santa's hat?"

She chuckled at whatever had just come to her mind, and he was glad it was a happy memory. "One year, Gran-gran and I decided to do a 'snow globe' theme. We got these little balloons that were see-through and poured some glitter inside, and then pushed in little random objects we found outside before blowing them up. We had thought it was the most genius idea ever until we put them on the tree and a good half of the balloons popped when they made contact with the pine needles. We were both laughing so hard, I don't think we even finished decorating it before the horn sounded."

Her story made him smile. Their lives growing up were so different from each other. He was glad she had memories like that.

"I'm worried that we aren't going to finish everything," Noelle said. "It's going to take a while to cut out all the snowflakes and glue ribbons to all the ornaments, so we need to get back as quickly as we can. I know where the paper is at The Crafty One. Do you want to run into Trove of Oldies and ask for the tissue paper at the same time?"

He said yes just as he turned into a parking spot, coming to a stop way too quickly, and they both jumped out of his car and ran into their stores. There must not have been too many people in line at The Crafty One because she actually beat him back out to the car. The woman at the Trove of Oldies register had wanted to hear all about the scavenger hunt, but still, it hadn't taken too long.

Then they drove back to Noelle's parents' house. The whole time they were in the car, he tried to think back to the last time when he'd done anything as fun as this and was coming up blank. Surely a race to gather supplies wasn't the highlight of his life.

He glanced over to where Noelle sat with such an intense look of determination on her face. Maybe it was less about what he was doing and more about who he was doing it with.

They parked, grabbed the supplies, and headed into the house. After they dumped all the supplies on the craft table, Noelle pulled out her phone. "Thirty-two minutes! I think we just set a record!"

It was a good thing they had twenty-eight minutes left on the timer instead of fifteen because his hands weren't used to doing stuff like this. They started with the pinecone and made the star for the top of the tree before realizing that they didn't have a way to make it stay up there. Noelle gasped, then ran out of the room. Moments later, she returned with a triumphant smile on her face, holding an empty toilet paper roll. "We'll just hot glue it to this, and then we can just slide it down over the top branch."

Surprisingly, it worked. They cut snowflakes out of the big tissue paper next, which wasn't easy. Then, side by side, they laid out the snowflakes on the floor, corners overlapping, and taped them together, and started bunching them and tying the bunched part with ribbons. They were working so closely that their shoulders were nearly constantly touching, their hands brushing each other with every ribbon they tied. And every time they did, it sent a new feeling of euphoria through him.

The same thing happened as they cut ribbons, glued them to the back of the star pretzels, and then cut little snowflakes from the shiny silver paper. It was too thick to fold and cut like Aiden had, so they quickly used the square and round hole punches to make it look as close as possible to snowflakes.

Then they went to work putting all their decorations on the tree. As they hung the garland, they pushed some of the lights through the holes in the thin paper, making it look like moonlight spilling over fresh snow. It amazed him how well they worked together, seeming to anticipate each other's moves, working so much more quickly than he could've guessed.

They got the final pretzel stars and silver snowflakes hung on the tree just as Noelle's mom called out, "Five-minute warning!"

Noelle turned to him, her breaths coming fast, a look of wonder on her face. "We finished with five minutes to spare! Can you believe it? And look how amazing our tree is!" She gave him a hug, and he gave her a tight squeeze back.

They both turned to admire their handiwork. He had to admit he was impressed that they could decorate the tree in the amount of time they had and make it look awesome. He felt taller just looking at it.

"We've got time," Noelle said. "Maybe we can get a few more lights to show through the garland."

They both leaned in, hands working together as they moved around the tree, this time without the sense of urgency that had driven them for the past hour. This time, he just reveled in being so close to Noelle, being so in sync with her.

On one particularly tough part, where the tape made the garland bunch up weird, they were both leaned in close, both of their hands bumping each other as they worked, and Noelle turned her face from the tree to his. He looked over, too, their faces barely a couple of inches apart. He could feel her quiet breath, smell her shampoo, which smelled remarkably like gingerbread, and see the longing in her eyes.

She was so beautiful. He'd known it for a long time. But now he understood how much of her beauty came from the person she was on the inside, shining through for all to see.

She bit her bottom lip, and his eyes were immediately drawn to those lips. Those lips that he'd imagined kissing a million times over, stopping himself each time. Then he saw her eyes shift to his lips, too.

Then, after a quick breath, Noelle's hands flew to his face, her palms resting against the sides of his face, her fingertips in his hair, and her lips were on his. He let out a slight groan, and they both straightened to standing as he put an arm around her waist, pulling her closer.

Her lips moved against his with the same sense of urgency they had felt while decorating the tree. A need to hurry before time ran out.

There's time, he thought. *We have time.*

And, just like they'd been in sync all evening, she seemed to be in sync with his thoughts, too. The sense of urgency seemed to flee, and she relaxed into the kiss, her fingers slowly skimming along his cheeks, down his neck, across his collarbone, her hands coming to rest on his shoulders.

A tiny voice said that he shouldn't be kissing her. But a much louder voice, one that only spoke in emotions, told him that this was perfect. She was perfect. Kissing her was perfect. That part of him exploded with hope, adoration, happiness, peace. A dream a year and a half in the making coming to life.

He was here with Noelle. And if he wasn't mistaking the emotions she seemed to be pouring into this kiss, she felt about him the same as he felt about her. Heat radiated through him, a lightness in his limbs, a tension-free calm spreading out from his chest.

"Time's up!" Noelle's mom called from the kitchen.

Noelle pulled away ever so slightly, and he traced kisses along her jaw, then paused with his lips just brushing her ear and whispered, "I think that means we should stop."

She sighed and sank into him, her body pressed against his, a hand resting on his chest, filling him full of light and heat. “There should be a trophy for *that* because I’m pretty sure we just won.”

He chuckled softly. “I think we did.”

As he heard the footsteps of walking adults and racing kids heading back to the central kitchen and family room area from all the places in the house they’d scattered to, that quiet voice inside him whispered just barely loud enough to be heard, *But you’re her boss.*

He ignored it as, hand-in-hand, they headed into the family room with everyone else.

CHAPTER ELEVEN

Noelle

Noelle got into her car Monday morning to go to work and blasted the *Christmas All Day* station, singing along to it. Christmas music just didn't sound the same in the rental car she'd been driving. She patted Elfie's dash. It was so good to have her back.

Christmas was five days away. Christmas Eve—and her birthday—was Friday. She loved her job, but it was still exciting to have a break coming up.

She took her usual detour to bypass driving through Main Street. She still hadn't recovered enough from Gran-gran's passing to drive down it with all its Christmas decorations yet—it still flooded her with too many emotions to handle first thing in the morning—but she was making progress. She only had four days of work this week before they were off for Christmas break, and she was determined to drive down it by Thursday morning.

And, because she hadn't gone a full five minutes since Saturday night without thinking about the kiss she and Jack shared, her mind went there again. All night long, they had worked together so well. So many times, they'd brushed hands, shoulders, knees. So many little touches from working so closely together, yet every one of them had sent thrills right through her.

As they were working on putting the final touches on their tree, he just looked at her with the sweetest expression. Like there was nowhere else he would rather be and no one else he'd rather be with. Like he was just soaking in the moment of being with her, and it mirrored what she felt so much that she'd wanted to kiss him so badly.

It had taken a lot of guts to make that move because she hadn't been sure how he would respond. The moment he put his arm around her waist and pulled her close, a weight had lifted from her, and she just sank into his kiss. It had been so sweet and wonderful and full of more emotions than she could even name.

She jerked out of the memory at the sound of her phone ringing. Glancing at the console, she could see that it was her sister, Hope. She pressed the button to let the car answer the phone. Elfie might not have power windows, but the manufacturer must've known how much she'd need Bluetooth.

"Hi, sis!"

"Hi! Okay, I just got Makelle off to school, and Porter and Weston are quietly eating breakfast, which means I have about a four-minute window of calmness here. Tell me about this weekend! You and Jack were looking pretty cozy. Did he kiss you? Because I got the vibe that he wanted to kiss you."

"I kissed him."

Hope squealed. "I knew it! When? How was it?"

"When we were decorating the tree, and it was *amazing*. It was like everything all night had been building up to it. Actually, everything from the moment he showed up to the hayride Friday night. We had just been on the same page so much the whole night, and I could tell that he wanted to kiss me as badly as I wanted to kiss him. It was magical. Like nothing I've ever experienced."

Hope squealed again, and she wasn't even a squealer. "That's how it was the first time Cory and I kissed. Tell me more. Was there a second kiss?"

"No." She'd tried to not sound disappointed when she said the word, but it came out anyway. "It just started seeming like we weren't on the same page so much after that. Like he was pulling away."

"Maybe he just didn't like the food. I mean, Julianne's team's chicken tortilla soup was pretty... interesting."

Noelle chuckled. "True. But I think it has more to do with him being my boss; I know he was worried about that. I was hoping that he'd kind of decided that it wasn't such a big deal. But I don't know, maybe I was wrong. And it wasn't like he was dropping any big hints that he's not okay with 'us.' It was more subtle things. Things I might not have picked up on if we hadn't been so in sync."

"Ooo, that's tough. Weston! We don't put fistfuls of Cheerios and milk in people's hair." She heard a few sounds of dishes moving and a grunt, probably as Hope pulled Weston out of his high chair, then heard the water run. "Keep talking. I'm listening."

"I just think I probably shouldn't have let my heart get so involved. I never thought that would even be an issue when Jack asked me to take this side job, so I was kind of blindsided by my attraction to him. I should just back away as quickly as possible."

"Maybe you should," Hope said, which she was totally not expecting, especially after the squeals.

"But my heart got involved with his nephew, too. I went over there yesterday after church to give him the star-shaped pretzels, and we just hung out and played. He's just such a cute kid. And I think he'll be sad, too. He has really loved playing with everyone's kids."

"Oh, yeah. That's extra tough."

"And I just can't stop thinking that when Christmas is over, Jack is going to go back to just being my boss, and Aiden is going to go back to being a kid I never see because it wasn't like I had seen him even once during the first year and a half I worked for Jack. And I'm not sure I can handle either of those things, Hope. Especially not the part about Jack."

"So, what do you want to do?"

"What do I *want* to do? I want to spend time with him outside of work every single day and then kiss like we did on Saturday night."

"Okay, so what are you *going* to do?"

"I don't know. We texted a bit yesterday, but even his texts seemed more distant."

"Maybe you should talk to Becca and Corbin since they've both worked in human resources."

"Maybe." She pulled into a parking spot in front of work. "I just need to put him out of my mind. I need to back away. Amazing kiss, amazing night, amazing man or not, I just need to back away before I get my heart in any deeper." She took in a long breath, then blew it out in a huff. "I just need to focus on being grateful that I have Elfie fixed, and I'm driving her again. That was what I did all this for in the first place. Mission accomplished."

"That sounds like a plan. Good luck with it!"

After Noelle went inside the building and set her bag at her desk, she pulled out her lunch container and headed to the break room to put it in the fridge.

As soon as she stepped through the doorway and saw Jack pouring himself a cup of coffee, she knew her plan was destined to fail, and no amount of luck was going to save it. It wasn't like she had started falling for him, and it was no big deal because she was actually bungee jumping and was going to get pulled back to the starting point at any minute. She had already fallen entirely. The parachute had been deployed, she'd landed, and there was no going back.

"Hi," she breathed, a smile spreading across her face.

A beautiful, perfect, joyful smile filled his face, too. How had she not been falling for this man from the moment she'd started working here?

The second he'd switched from his natural reaction at seeing her to a logical, thought-out worry was evident on his face. She knew that something along the lines of "I'm the boss, so this isn't appropriate" was churning in his mind. But she could also see hints of something else. The same longing that she was feeling. She wanted to tell that part of him to stay strong. She really wanted it to win.

"Good morning."

"How was the rest of your weekend?"

He opened his mouth like he was going to give the answer that first came to mind, but then he shut it again. Then he said slowly, pausing after every word or two like he was choosing his words with great care. "It was... good. I can't say it came without worries."

Oh, no. He had definitely been spending a lot of time thinking about the boss/employee thing. In an attempt to keep things light, she put on a big smile and said, "It sounds like you need a night of Christmas fun to keep your mind off your worries."

He just studied her, not responding, and she could see the care in his eyes. Then his eyes shifted to the door behind her, and he turned back to his coffee. Noelle turned around just in time to see Lennox, who had strode into the room, falter in his step as he looked between the two of them, trying to decipher what had just been going on.

Noelle acted like nothing was out of the ordinary and opened the fridge, putting her lunch inside. "The meeting's at two-thirty, right?" There. She'd just made it sound like that's all they'd been talking about.

Jack nodded, then gave Lennox a nod and said, "Good morning," then walked out of the break room.

Lennox clearly hadn't bought her "Let's talk about the meeting" cover. Probably because the meeting was always at 2:30 on Mondays.

He glanced at the doorway Jack had left through then back at Noelle. "So, what was that about?"

"Just an issue with a client and my part in it." She didn't mention that Jack was the client. And she definitely didn't say that her part in it had been falling in love with him.

Since she'd thrown herself under the bus with the comment, Lennox seemed to buy it. He grimaced. "That's no fun. Good luck."

That was twice in less than twenty minutes she'd been wished luck on something that needed more than luck. It wasn't like Jack was going to stop being her boss, and it didn't appear that her heart was going to stop wanting a relationship with him.

CHAPTER TWELVE

Jack

Jack went back into his office, shut the door behind him, set his coffee on his desk, then ran his fingers through his hair. The moment Noelle had walked through the doorway into the break room, his entire body had filled with happiness. Like it had forgotten all the time he'd spent worrying over the past day and a half. His body just felt more alive whenever she was in the same room.

But Lennox's reaction to catching them in the teeniest tiniest bit of a moment together was precisely the reason why it was so wrong to have fallen so fully for Noelle.

He knew Friday that he'd stepped over a line in the sand that he'd drawn for himself. He'd known then that the smart thing to do—the responsible thing to do—would've been to call things off then. Yet he didn't.

And then, during Saturday's activity, there had been no time to think—just time to react as they raced through the scavenger hunt and made everything they needed for the tree. There hadn't been time for the logical part of him to keep shouting that he was making a wrong choice. He was usually so good at self-discipline. How had he let himself get into a situation with such considerable consequences to his heart?

And now that he was looking back, he realized he had been brushing over that line and redrawing it for a couple of weeks. Opening himself up more and more to Noelle.

He sank into the chair behind his desk and couldn't stop thinking about the way Noelle's face had lit up when she walked into the break room. And what it did to his stomach to see the woman he'd been falling in love with for the past year and a half having such a joyful response at seeing him.

Which made him think about the look she'd had on her face right before she had kissed him. He wanted to experience seeing that look on her face every day.

But then, like all the emotions had been standing in line to see him, the moment that one stepped away, the next one he'd experienced that night stepped forward. After their kiss, he and Noelle had joined the rest of her big family to see the results of everyone's Mystery Santa Hat offerings.

And as he stood, surrounded by all of them, he thought about how much he'd been falling for Noelle's family, too. They were everything he had grown up without. Rachel and Aiden meant everything to him. He never would've guessed that his heart had room for a family that big, but then they went and surprised him, too, and showed him how much he actually needed them. He saw it in Rachel's face during the hayride and Aiden's every time they did anything at Noelle's parents' house.

And all of that scared him. Because he was still Noelle's boss, which meant that he *couldn't* have a relationship with her.

All through that night, the emotions within him battled. He sat at Noelle's side as Becca, Corbin, and their four little kids performed a sweet version of the first Christmas, with Joseph wearing a colander as a hat, Mary wearing a Superman cape, a shepherd wearing a bedazzled scarf instead of robes and holding a stuffed bear instead of a sheep, a wise man wearing a suit coat that was so long on her that it dragged on the floor, a second wise man wearing swim goggles and arm floaties, and baby Jesus constantly climbing out of the giant mixing bowl that was supposed to be the manger. The wise men placed gifts of gold, frankincense, and myrrh at baby Jesus's manger, but were actually a mixing cup, a microphone from a preschooler's karaoke machine, and a lint roller that baby Jesus kept trying to put in his mouth.

And then they watched as Katie and her date reenacted the scene from the movie Elf when he sang, "I'm singing! I'm in a store, and I'm singing!" Her date played the part of Buddy the Elf, and Katie played the roles of Jovie, the store manager, and several people in the store, hurrying to change costumes and props with each line.

Laughter had filled him as they watched both skits, loving sitting next to Noelle and being with all her family. Yet, sadness that it all was going to go away had quickly fought with that laughter.

He'd been so proud of their tree when they presented it. With as overwhelmed as he'd felt by the task, it had turned out well. Of course, Hope's family had turned theirs into a "family tree," with each family member hand-drawn by their kids, and had taken home the trophy. Still, though, he'd been impressed by the tree he and Noelle had made.

There had been a lot more laughter—and plenty of "*Eww!*" and "Gross!" and even a few people said "Yum!" as they ate the creations from the two teams who had pulled "Dinner" from Santa's hat.

Julianne, along with her husband and two kids, had made chicken tortilla soup that definitely had chicken in it, and he guessed some taco seasoning, but the rest of the soup looked like it was maybe four different kinds of canned soup mixed together. Their dessert was an Oreo cookie topped with a dollop of Cool Whip, topped with a single blueberry. It was kind of weird, but not too bad.

Noelle's parents had made a stir fry with a strange collection of vegetables and a meat that was definitely *not* chicken. His guess was canned tuna. They'd made an apple crisp that was pretty impressive, especially considering that the topping seemed to be made out of a mix of crushed potato chips, Fritos, and Doritos.

And he'd experienced it all with Noelle by his side. During it all, things were slightly awkward between them and didn't have the same easiness they had gained during their previous activities. He knew it was all coming from him because grief at the impending loss battled with contented happiness all night long. Yet, he still longed to spend every moment with her. Even knowing that every minute spent with her was going to make calling it all off even more difficult.

He stood up and paced in his office, trying to come to terms with what he needed to do, especially when such a large part of him was fighting every bit of it.

But if Saturday night hadn't let him know that he needed to end things, Sunday night did. He'd gone over to Rachel's for dinner and to check on them, and Aiden couldn't stop talking about how Noelle had come over and played with him and how much fun he had.

Somehow, he hadn't thought through how much hiring Noelle would affect his nephew. Of course he'd get attached to her. Who wouldn't? How could he not have realized that?

He was in deep. They all were. He needed to end things before it got any worse.

CHAPTER THIRTEEN

Noelle

Noelle's workload of last-minute ad copy changes for the final days of Christmas advertising was huge. She spent all morning intensely focused on them, then hit it again hard after lunch. By two, her brain was mush, so she leaned back in her chair and ran her hands over her face.

Then she opened her desk drawer and pulled out the tin of cards from Gran-gran. She ran the tips of her fingers over the scene Gran-gran had painted of the two of them standing in front of the little tree they'd decorated with balloon snow globes, half of them popped, holding their stomachs from laughing so hard.

It was a great memory.

So was Saturday night's.

If Gran-gran had been there, she would've been hooting and slapping her knee and wiping tears from her eyes from laughing so hard at the skits. During the dinner, she would've been giving commentary on the meal like she was a food critic at a Michelin-starred restaurant, saying how delectable everything was. And she would've said that the tree she and Jack decorated should be on display in the White House.

She carefully placed the card back in the tin and put the one with the pet costume parade leaning against her monitor. The painting on it was of when they had dressed Gran-gran's dog, Daisy, up as a Christmas tree with a star on her head. They were going to do something similar tonight with Aiden's dog, Bailey. She had already dropped off at Rachel's and Aiden's house a big piece of green felt, colored pom-poms, ribbon that looked like it could be used as a garland, and her hot glue gun.

Bridget rolled her chair over to Noelle's desk. "Remember how I didn't have a clue what to get my mom for Christmas? Well, her little dog apparently decided she was mad about something and took it out on my mom's favorite lap blanket. So I went to that store in the mall with all the comfort items and got her the softest blanket I've ever seen."

"Oh! Jack got his sister one of those blankets! I couldn't believe how soft it was."

Bridget cocked her head to the side, a mix of confusion and something else on her face. Suspicion? "You went shopping with Jack?" She paused a moment, then added, "Is that the after-hours job he was asking for a volunteer to take in the meeting a couple of weeks ago?"

Noelle nodded. "Well, actually, it was all about doing Christmassy things with his five-year-old nephew, Aiden.

His sister is sick and can't do it herself. But since he hates Christmas, he wanted help."

Bridget nodded slowly.

She hadn't meant to keep it a secret from her coworkers. They just hadn't asked, and she hadn't thought to bring it up. But she fully intended to keep the kiss a secret. But even though she would've had no problem talking about it last week or the week before, she felt weird talking with Bridget about it now, especially because of all the feelings she was having about him.

"How's that going?"

"Good!" Her voice came out bright, just like she'd hoped. She hoped it came out with zero guilt, too. "He's a super cute kid. He's helped me to reconnect with Gran-gran."

"Aww. That's so sweet. Then I'm glad it was you who agreed to help."

Noelle really didn't want the conversation to continue, just in case she asked any tough questions. So she said, "Have you created the images yet for the Ducasse account? I'm having trouble coming up with ad copy for them and could use some inspiration." The topic change totally worked, and she did a mental fist pump.

By the time she got everything together that she needed for their staff meeting, most of her coworkers had already headed to the conference room. Arms full of papers, notebooks, and her tablet, she headed down the hall leading to the meeting. Jack stood outside of the door, greeting people as they entered, like he always did, standing tall and looking so incredible and professional in his navy suit. It was such a different look than what she saw him wear outside of work, yet he was every bit as attractive both ways.

A wide smile spread across her face at seeing him. She expected a similar return smile from him, but instead, he just gave a nod and said, "Noelle."

She walked into the meeting and found a seat, wondering if he was losing interest or if he was just so much better at hiding their relationship at work than she was. She hoped it was the latter because a forbidden relationship was kind of exciting. That, and it made her heart hurt to even think that he wasn't interested.

Which was stupid, because she'd already decided to back away and keep her heart protected.

He was acting so distant all through the meeting, though, which made her start questioning everything. He'd always been distant at work, so that part wasn't entirely unusual. He just hadn't been quite so distant since she started seeing him outside of work to help with Aiden.

And then, completely unbidden, their kiss popped into her mind. He had definitely been on the same page as her during that kiss. They had definitely connected on a new level Friday and Saturday. Seeing him acting like nothing had happened—even if that was the way he should be acting while at work—made her realize just how much she'd fallen for him.

She was the last one to gather her things at the end of the meeting, and as she passed by Jack at the door, she said, "Are we still on for the pet parade tonight?" After seeing how he'd been in the meeting, she'd started to wonder if they were.

"Aiden is really looking forward to it."

She nodded, wondering exactly what that meant. She had gotten about three steps down the hall when he said, "Noelle, can you meet with me in my office at four?"

She turned and said, "Sure," then headed back to her desk.

There was still a lot she needed to get done by the end of the day. But at least half of her brain was constantly wondering why he wanted to see her in his office. Should she be excited because he was going to sneak a kiss when no one in the office was looking? Or should she be worried that his acting distant was a foreshadowing of what was to come?

At four o'clock on the dot, she knocked on his office door, and he immediately opened it, then closed it behind her. He motioned to the couch that sat against one wall—the one she'd never seen him use. So she sat down and studied his face. There was no "I'm about to kiss you like we kissed Saturday night and make your entire week" look on his face. All that was there was a seriousness. A sense of determination.

"I have...worries. About"—he glanced at the door—"Saturday night. Worries about myself, I guess. I don't think it's a good idea for me to be around you outside of work."

Just the thought of not seeing him outside of work made her feel like she was going to crumble. She could talk big with Hope, and she could even talk big to herself and mostly convince herself that it was for the best. But the fact remained that she had completely fallen for him. Enough that it sounded miserable to not have him in her life outside of being her boss.

Okay, Noelle. Think about this logically. He said he was worried about Saturday, so the kissing her part. He hadn't mentioned all the other days. "Let's just assume that Saturday happened because Aiden wasn't there. He'll be there tonight, so it'll be just fine."

"I don't think it'll be fine. Aiden's presence hasn't stopped me from wanting to be around you yet."

So he was interested in her. Somehow, though, the knowledge of that made this all even more heartbreaking. Could he not get over the fact that he was her boss? She swallowed hard and tried to be strong. "I can take Aiden to the pet costume parade tonight without you." That was what their original pact had been, anyway.

He shook his head. "I don't think that's going to work, either. I'm sorry. I know tonight is important to him, so I'll help him make the costume for Bailey and take them to the costume parade. But I think we should mark our agreement as fulfilled. I will still pay you the amount we agreed upon, of course, but your help is no longer needed."

CHAPTER FOURTEEN

Jack

A massive weight seemed to be dragging Jack down as he drove from Golden to his sister's house in Mountain Springs. All he wanted to do was bury himself in work, sleep, run a few miles, or do anything else that would keep him from having all of his thoughts directed at Noelle and how he'd ended things. And to keep his mind off how his heart was aching at the thought of things going back to the way they'd been before he'd asked for her help.

If they could even go back to that.

But he knew how much tonight meant to Aiden, and he wasn't about to go back on his word to him. When he walked into Rachel's house, Aiden did his customary run down the hallway and leaped onto him, giving him a starfish hug. He hugged Aiden back, then set him back on the floor. "Where's your mom?"

"In here," Rachel said, her voice sounding weak.

He walked into the kitchen to see her carrying a bowl to the sink, looking like she didn't have the energy to even stay standing long enough to get to a chair. He rushed to her side. "Are you okay? What do you need? Do you need me to take you to the hospital?"

She shook her head. "I'm just so tired today. That's all."

"Then you should sleep. Do you need anything before going to bed?"

"No. But I was going to..."

He put an arm around her back to support her. "I know. But do you think you have the energy for that?"

She sighed, seeming resigned. So he scooped her into his arms and carried her into her bedroom, and placed her gently on her bed. "Where's your phone?"

"On the table, I think."

Aiden had followed them into the bedroom, so he asked him to run out and get his mom's phone. When he got back, he laid it on the nightstand beside her. "Just sleep. Don't worry about anything. Aiden and I are going to have a great time tonight. I'll wake you up when I bring him back home and get him to bed."

"Are you sure you don't need anything right now?"

"I'm sure."

"Call or text me if you do need anything, okay?"

She nodded. He gave her hand a squeeze, and Aiden pushed into the space between them and gave his mom a tight hug. "I'll tell you all about the parade later, okay?"

She kissed Aiden on the forehead, and Jack led him out of the room.

The two of them looked at the bag of supplies that Noelle had dropped off that they somehow had to make a dog costume out of. He was already feeling lost without Noelle and was hoping that Rachel would be feeling great and could give them some direction.

"Well, buddy," he said, "it looks like it's up to us to figure this out."

"When is Noelle going to get here?"

This was the question he'd been dreading. "She's not going to be here. I'm sorry."

Aiden let out a breath that made his chest sink and his shoulders slump. "Will she be at the costume parade?"

He shook his head. "I don't know."

They moved the coffee table in the family room off to the side then emptied the bag's contents onto the floor. The little colored puffs were obviously meant to be ornaments, and the ribbon, he was guessing, was probably a garland. Oh, and there was a hot glue gun; he plugged that into the outlet and put it on the coffee table. He was glad he found out how that worked on Saturday night. But the two foot square of green felt? He didn't have a clue what to do with that.

"Well, where do you think we should start?"

"Noelle didn't tell you how we make it?"

He shook his head. He hadn't even thought to ask.

Aiden tapped a finger on his lip, thinking, a mannerism that always made Jack smile. Aiden grabbed hold of the felt and turned it, smoothing it out. "We should make it a diamond, like this, instead of a square. Maybe this point at the top can be the top of the Christmas tree, then these points at the side can wrap around onto Bailey's stomach."

He was impressed at the kid's ability to figure this out. "Come here, girl," he said to Bailey, and the dog walked right over to him like she was all-in on this project. He and Aiden laid the fabric on Bailey's back, and Aiden pressed the sides down and held them in place under Bailey's stomach. Okay, that could work.

"And then maybe we should just cut this bottom point off," Aiden said, marking it with his hand, "so it's flat, like the bottom of a tree."

He nodded and spread the fabric out on the floor. He handed the scissors to Aiden and said, "Do you want to do the honors?"

Aiden grinned and started cutting as Jack drew a line with his finger just ahead of Aiden's cut. It was an extremely jagged line, but Christmas trees were like that, anyway. And Aiden was so proud of it.

He looked at the ribbon and pom-poms, then to the glue gun. "This glue gets really hot, so I think I better do that part. Do you want to just choose an item, I'll glue it, then you point where to put it?"

Aiden nodded, and they went to work. Aiden hadn't exactly had the same picture in his mind as Jack did about how the ribbon should go on, but he let him make it his own. In the end, the ribbon went in wavy lines in three crisscrossing directions, and pom-poms were stuck everywhere.

Aiden sat back on his heels, surveying their work, and grinned. Then he put out a fist, and Jack bumped it with his.

Then he looked down at his hands in his lap. "I really wish Noelle had come. I miss her."

"I do, too, buddy." So much.

Aiden nodded and reached out to scratch the top of Bailey's golden head. "Do you want to try this on? Stand up, girl."

Bailey complied, and they laid the fabric on her a second time. It looked better than Jack thought it would. But then Bailey barked and wiggled her back in excitement, and the tree costume fell right off.

"It needs to connect," Aiden said. "How do we do that part?

"I don't know," Jack admitted. They couldn't exactly use hot glue to glue it into place without endangering Bailey or one of them. Plus, he didn't know if they'd be able to get the costume off after that.

"Can we tie it?"

Jack tried, but it wasn't quite long enough for a knot. He also had the idea to pull off one of the pom-poms and glue it to one point underneath and cut a slit in the other point to use it as a button, but he'd apparently used way too much glue on the pom-poms to be able to remove one.

"I really miss Noelle," Aiden said again.

"She made stuff like this look easy, didn't she?" He hadn't fully appreciated that trait of hers until just then. He looked down at his watch. They needed to leave within the next minute or two if they wanted a chance of being there in time.

"Oh!" Jack said, bunching the fabric at Bailey's stomach in his hand. "We could just use a rubber band to hold it like this! Do you know if you have one?"

Aiden jumped up and ran to a drawer in their kitchen and started rifling through it. "What about this?" he asked, holding up a hairband.

"Perfect."

Bailey was remarkably patient as they tried with the costume once again. The hair tie worked, and the outfit looked like it might stay in place for a bit. Hopefully for long enough.

"Okay, run and get your shoes and coat on. I'll get Bailey's leash."

Ten minutes later, they pulled into a parking spot at the community center and ran with Bailey and her costume to get inside. Pets dressed in all kinds of Christmas costumes and their owners were everywhere, and Jack had to work to keep Aiden and Bailey at his side while he checked in. Then someone led them to a room beside the gym to get Bailey's costume on.

It was less easy getting the hair tie holding the costume on this time around because Bailey was so excited to be around all the people and other dogs who shared the room. But eventually, they managed to, not long before someone came in.

"Okay, listen up. You're Dogs Group Two. I want you all to file in behind me. I will lead you through the parade route, and then you'll be free to come back here to get anything you left behind, or you can join the folks sitting to watch the parade."

She led them back to the gym, where everyone sat in the middle of the room while all the dogs paraded around the perimeter. Instead of looking at the other dogs, every minute that his eyes weren't on Aiden and Bailey, they were scanning the crowd for Noelle, desperately hoping to catch even a glimpse of her.

But they made the circuit around the room, and he couldn't see her at all. They found seats and sat down while Aiden told Bailey over and over how good she did and how proud he was of her.

Maybe Noelle was bringing her parents' dog to the show. His mind raced with all the things he could say to her and what it would be like seeing her. He wondered if they were ever going to be able to get things back to the professional relationship they'd had before.

And he spent plenty of time cursing himself for ever letting his feelings take the driver's seat. She was his employee, and he'd decided long ago when he first started being attracted to her that he was never going to let anything happen. And then he did and ruined everything.

He shouldn't have been surprised, though. How could he not fall in love with her by spending time outside of the office with her? Still, he should've made different choices. He owned the company, so it wasn't like he could stop being her boss.

His heart leaped when he spotted Noelle's parents walk into the gym with their black lab, Captain, at their side, dressed as Rudolph and pulling a tiny sleigh. It took a bit for them to make their way around all four sides of the gym and to where he was sitting, but when they got close, he stood up and went to them to say hello. They said hello to Aiden and Bailey, too, and said how much they liked her costume.

"Is Noelle here?" Feelings of hope were caught in his chest.

But they both gave sad shakes of their heads. Then her mom said, "Her gran-gran had a little tan and white terrier named Daisy, and Noelle and Gran-gran used to work together on a costume and dress her up every year for this event. Daisy passed not long after Gran-gran did —this is our first Christmas without her. Between that and..." She didn't say whatever came after the "and," but it was clear that she meant Jack ending things earlier today. She cleared her throat. "Well, it was just too much."

He closed his eyes for a quick moment. He'd stopped things right before an activity that was probably already so difficult for her. He didn't want her to feel bad and wished he could go to her and comfort her without making things worse. "Is she okay?"

Her dad lifted a shoulder in a shrug. "Not yet, but she will be."

Her mom reached out and gave his hand a squeeze, looking at him like she was trying to impart something to him. Courage? Hope? Forgiveness? He wasn't sure. All he knew was that it wasn't a look of harsh judgment like he deserved. "It's good to see you, Jack, Aiden, Bailey. I hope we get to see you around again soon."

As they turned and left, he suddenly remembered their Christmas Eve plans, which also happened to be Noelle's birthday plans. He, Aiden, and Rachel had all been invited to the big dinner and celebration. It hadn't hit him until just now that he was ruining Rachel's and Aiden's Christmas Eve plans, too. And he ended things with Noelle just days before her birthday.

He'd gotten them all into quite a mess, and he had no idea how to get them out. He ran his hands over his face.

Aiden tugged on his coat. "Why is Noelle not okay?"

"It's just been a really tough couple of days, buddy."

He nodded like he understood. Then he said, "Well, then we should do something to make things better."

"I know. I just wish I knew how."

CHAPTER FIFTEEN

Noelle

Noelle rolled over in bed and looked at the clock on her phone. She really needed to get up and get ready for work. Could she call in sick? No. She'd sent an email to everyone at work—all eight of them, including Jack—to say that she was ill on Tuesday, which she never did. She loved her job too much for taking time off. But her heart hurt enough that she definitely hadn't been well enough to go in.

She still felt like she wasn't.

She had thought of letting everyone know that she was sick yesterday, too, but her workload was too big to skip a second day. And since today was the final day before Christmas break, she really had to go in. She couldn't leave all of her work for her co-workers. So she forced herself to get out of bed and to get ready.

She knew she had promised herself to drive down Main Street by today, but she just couldn't. Not now.

Her birthday was tomorrow, and she was going to be twenty-six. She had kind of figured that she would be married by now. Maybe even thinking about having a kid.

Not still single. And the first guy she had been interested in for quite a while was completely unattainable.

Not that it was a reason for being sad about her age or thinking she hadn't accomplished things. She probably wouldn't have even thought about it at all if it wasn't for the fact that she had fallen for Jack so entirely and wanted him in her life.

Her workday ended up mostly being the same today as it had been yesterday. She'd tried to pretend that everything was fine, but everyone seemed to know that she wasn't okay. And it wasn't just Bridget and Lennox who had noticed. She had mostly managed to avoid Jack at work, but apparently, he had been pretending that everything was fine and failing at it, too, because everyone was talking about it.

And although they weren't saying anything, they were definitely putting two and two together and realizing that her and Jack being simultaneously *not fine* probably meant that they weren't fine because of each other.

Noon rolled around, which meant it was time for their Holiday Sendoff celebration. They all headed into the conference as their catered meal was brought in, and everyone prepared to socialize before taking off work and doing whatever it was that they were doing for the holidays. She couldn't avoid Jack there.

They all took seats around the big conference table that they usually had meetings at like it was a big family dinner, both Jack and Noelle pretending to be fine. But there was a tension in the air surrounding everyone.

After they all dished up their food, she attempted to lighten the mood by saying, "How about we go around the table and tell our favorite something. Like our favorite holiday song or holiday movie."

"Or our favorite person to spend the holiday with," Lennox said, clearly attempting to decipher the situation.

"No," Jack said with enough authority that it left no room for negotiation.

"Oh…kay," Lennox said. "Favorite movie, then."

As they went around the table, saying what their favorite movie was, Jack looked across the table at her with a longing that matched her own.

If they felt the same way about each other, it was stupid that they should both be miserable and apart. She pulled out her phone and texted her sister, Becca.

> NOELLE: Can I come over after work and talk with you and Corbin?

> BECCA: Of course! Come at 6:00 if you want dinner, 7:30 if you want ice cream.

Noelle put a spoonful of ice cream in her mouth and savored the candy cane-flavored goodness as Corbin got their one-year-old out of her high chair, and Becca used a cloth to wipe all the ice cream off their three-year-old's mouth before he ran off to be crazy with their two older kids. Then her sister and brother-in-law joined her at the table in their beautiful home, the halls fully decked, Christmas music playing over the speakers, each of them finally getting to their bowls of ice cream.

Corbin got a scoop of ice cream on his spoon, then looked at it for a moment and said, "I'm guessing you're here about your boss," before he put the ice cream in his mouth.

Becca added, "And you're wanting our opinions on dating him since we've both worked in human resource departments."

"Wow, you guys are smart."

"That's why they pay us the big bucks," Becca said, winking.

"Okay, then, I have a question. Is it illegal for a boss to date an employee?"

"Illegal?" Corbin asked. "No. But it might be against your employment contract and could get you fired."

"It's not in my employment contract. So couldn't we just date?"

"What does he think about it?" Becca asked.

"He thinks we shouldn't. Like it's an ironclad law that shouldn't be broken. But I know that he really wants to date—I can see it in the way he looks at me. And I want to date him, so I just don't think we should let obstacles stand in our way."

Becca's eyebrow rose. "Does he seem like the kind of guy who would go against his beliefs to get what he wanted?"

Noelle let out a long breath. "No. Not even a little bit."

"Overcoming obstacles in a relationship is a good thing. So is respecting what's really important to the other person. He obviously cares a lot about his company—and he should! He's got what? Seven employees?"

"Eight."

"They all depend on him to make good choices for his company. He depends on it, too."

"I just don't see how our dating would be bad for the company."

"Okay, look at it this way," Corbin said. "If the two of you dated and fell in love and didn't keep it a secret, how would all of your coworkers feel about it?"

She thought about it for a moment. It had been a natural instinct to keep things with Jack quiet at work. Was it because she didn't believe her coworkers would be thrilled to know that they were dating? Both Bridget and Lennox had acted a little wary at the slightest hint that there was something between them.

"And how would you feel when you got a raise or a promotion or anything like that—maybe something you had been working hard for since the day you started working there—and everyone assumed that you only got it because you were dating the boss?"

Oh. Yeah, that wouldn't be awesome. She hadn't thought about that.

"Jack is smart to have strict rules for himself about dating one of his employees," Becca said. "Just think about breakups—they can get messy. And if they do, they can take a company down. But not only that, it can be nearly impossible to keep away from the appearance of favoritism. Even if someone is determined to not show favoritism, it can creep in without them even noticing. And that can greatly affect the morale of all the employees."

Noelle leaned back in her chair, stunned. She hadn't thought about any of those things at all. Ever since Jack had told her the story about how he'd never looked at his parents' marriage and felt that he wanted that for himself someday, she had kind of assumed that he was letting fear stop him. She covered her face with her hands. "I judged the situation so wrongly."

Then she sat up straight, dropping her hands from her face. "And I was the one to kiss him. I initiated that. The hand holding on the hayride, too. He had said that he couldn't get involved with me after the hayride, but I ignored that and still kissed him the next day."

Becca reached out and gave Noelle's hand a squeeze. "There was a lot you didn't know at the time. You can't beat yourself up for that. Plus, I think he might have been letting his heart take charge a bit, too."

"Maybe." She ran her spoon through and through her ice cream, making designs in the partially melted cream but not really seeing them. "But I do have the power to change things."

Corbin cocked his head to the side. "Are you talking about your job? You *love* your job."

"I do. But if you think about it, it all comes down to one question: which do I love more—my job or Jack?"

CHAPTER SIXTEEN

Jack

Jack walked into the office, unlocking doors and turning on lights as he went. Yes, it was Christmas Eve. No, he hadn't planned to work. But there was work here he could do, and he couldn't be at home all day, thoughts of how many people's Christmas Eve he'd ruined running on a loop.

Or how he had managed to find the perfect woman, the only one he'd ever imagined having a life with, the one who made his entire being happy to be alive, yet lose her just as they were getting started.

Or how he wanted to spend every single occasion with her—extraordinary or ordinary—but he had closed himself off from celebrating Christmas Eve and her birthday with her.

Or was he just not looking deeply enough for a solution? He wandered through the main office area, running his fingers along each of the desks as he meandered. Maybe he could hire a manager to run the day-to-day business, and he could take a step back. Could he give all of this up? Not be a part of it all? Could he find someone who would care about the business as much as he did? And if he did, could he pay them as much as they would be asking?

As he was thinking through the logistics, a thought popped into his mind. *Even if you did, you would still be her boss.*

A frustrated growl escaped his mouth. There had to be a way. He couldn't experience a glimpse of what life would be like with Noelle and then just live life without her. She had changed him. Now that he knew what was possible, he knew he couldn't turn his back on her. He had to find a way.

He turned to head back to his office, then stopped at Noelle's desk. A single hand-painted card was leaning against her monitor. He picked it up to get a closer look—it must be one of the cards she'd received from her gran-gran. He couldn't believe she'd left it there over the break. A woman—probably her gran-gran—was with someone who had to be Noelle. Christmas decorations filled the background of the scene. Noelle held in front of her a big cupcake with a lit candle on it. Her cheeks were full of air, her lips making an O as she was preparing to blow out the candle.

He turned the card over.

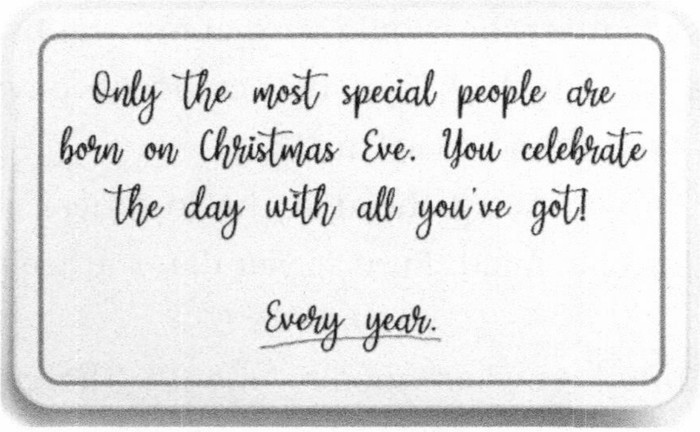
Only the most special people are born on Christmas Eve. You celebrate the day with all you've got!
Every year.

He put the card back and went into his office.

An hour later, not only had he not come up with a solution, but he had barely made a dent in the emails he was trying to get through. His senses went on high alert when he heard what he thought was a door opening. None of his employees worked today, and the building's cleaning staff wasn't in, either.

He was just standing up to go check on everything when Noelle appeared in his office doorway. "I thought I might find you here."

"Noelle. Why are you at work today?"

She stepped forward and held out an envelope. "I just came to give you this."

He took it from her hand but didn't so much as glance down at it—he didn't want to take his eyes off hers. "What is it?"

"My resignation letter."

Oh, no. Had he messed up so badly that he made her want to quit? "You know I can't accept this."

"I need you to."

He swallowed, afraid to ask the question but needing to anyway. "Why?"

"Because I think I might be in love with you."

He was too stunned to move.

"And I think that you might have been feeling the same things over the past few weeks, too."

"I've been feeling them over the past year and a half." The words were quiet. He couldn't believe they actually came out of his mouth.

Her eyebrows shot up. "A *year and a half*? Why didn't you ever tell me?" She paused. "Oh. Right. Because you are my boss." She gave a single nod like maybe pieces in her head were clicking into place. "Which is exactly why I need you to accept my resignation. Because now that I know what it's like to have you in my life, I don't want you to ever not be in my life."

Emotions pricked at his eyes. "I can't ask you to do that." He set the letter on his desk.

"Ahh, but you're not asking me, so it's okay."

"It's not, Noelle. You can't just quit your job for me. I'll —"

"Jack," she said, stepping forward and putting a hand on his forearm. "I appreciate you being all chivalrous and wanting to fix this, but you can't. It's *impossible* for you to fix this. Sure, you could be the one to quit, but then I would still be out of a job, and so would the seven other people who work here. Or you could change who you are as a person and ignore your rules about dating an employee, but I don't want you to change. I love you exactly how you are."

She took another small step forward. "But it's not impossible for me to fix it."

He looked down at the envelope on his desk, running a finger over the corner of it. He hadn't expected this at all and was so not mentally prepared for it. "You're the best ad copywriter that we've ever had."

"But I'm not the best one there is, so you're going to find someone else, and they're going to be awesome. Now here are the terms of my resignation. I'm not giving a two-week notice because I don't want to wait that long to see you again. But feel free to hire me as an independent contractor for two weeks to cover my job while you find someone new if you'd like. I'll be my own boss then, so there won't be any boss/employee anything going on."

He chuckled and shook his head, looking down at the ground. Could this really work? And if it did, would he always feel guilty that she had to leave because of him? "So you haven't started looking for another job yet?"

"Um, it's Christmas Eve."

"What if you don't find something?"

"Jack, I've been copywriting since I was old enough to talk. I'm going to find something quickly. Trust that I'm strong enough and capable enough to make this choice."

"I've seen you work, and I've seen you play. I know that you're more than strong enough and capable enough."

She smiled, and there was something else behind it. A playfulness. A confidence. Maybe even adoration. "You've got my resignation letter. It's up to you to choose whether to accept it or not. I'll know your answer by whether or not you show up for Christmas Eve dinner tonight."

Then she turned and walked to the doorway. She stopped right before going through it and turned her head just enough for him to see her cheekbone. "But tell Rachel and Aiden that they're welcome to come whether or not you do."

And then she left, and he stood there in the middle of his office, grinning so big it made his entire body happy.

CHAPTER SEVENTEEN

Noelle

Noelle finished spooning the seasoned panko breadcrumbs on the brie-stuffed mushrooms, then glanced in the direction of the front door for the fiftieth time. She wasn't only glancing when she heard people come in or out anymore—she was glancing every time she thought of Jack, which was about every four seconds, apparently.

"Ugh," Makelle, Hope's six-year-old daughter, said as she tried to turn the strips of pie crust dough into a lattice but kept getting mixed up on which one should be pulled back for another one to be laid down beneath it. "This is so hard!"

Noelle wiped off her hands on her apron. "Would you like some help?"

Makelle held up her hand like a stop sign. "No. You can't help with your own birthday cake! Besides, my mom says it's good to struggle because that's what helps you to grow. And I really want to be taller because this girl in my class, Trisha, has me beat, and she's not even nice. Don't worry—I've got this."

Noelle chuckled and glanced in the direction of the door again. Still no Jack. The place looked amazing, though. The big tree in the family room never looked better. Garlands were hung over every doorway, every side table and the mantle was decorated, the gingerbread train was moving around its tracks, Christmas music was playing over the speakers, and all of her family was surrounding her.

She should feel like she had everything she needed. But there was a particular pang of longing. A hole that wasn't filled. And that hole was Jack-sized.

"He'll come," Hope said as she reached around Noelle to grab the tray of mushrooms to slide them into the oven. "He has to."

She set the timer on the oven and took a breath. Based on their conversation in his office earlier today, she knew he would come. So why was she so nervous that he wouldn't?

"Happy birthday to Noelle," her five-year-old niece, Sadie, shouted out.

A chorus of voices shouted in return, "And to Noelle, a good night!"

Noelle grinned, held onto her Santa hat with *birthday girl* stitched into it, and took a slight bow as Sadie giggled.

Noelle went over to the big dining room table and helped Julianne to set it. She loved setting the table for this meal because they used the special white Christmas plates with the red rims, the white tablecloths, the red napkins with the red and white striped rings, the fancy crystal goblets, and the greenery down the center of the table that she and Gran-gran had picked out together.

She wished she hadn't left the cards from Gran-gran at work. She wanted them home with her, especially over Christmas. She'd realized she'd forgotten them at the end of work the day before and had meant to grab them when she'd gone to give Jack her letter of resignation earlier today, but she'd had so many other thoughts in her head then that she'd forgotten. And it wasn't like she could've just gone back at that point and seen Jack again after the way she left things.

The doorbell rang and her seven-year-old niece, Erika, jumped up to go get the door. She heard adult shoes stomping off snow, so she hurried over to the side of the family room by the stairs so she could see down the short hallway to the front door.

It was Rachel and Aiden, brushing snow out of their hair and off their coats before they stepped inside. She stood on her toes and peered around them but didn't see Jack. Erika said, "You can put your coats right there," and pointed to the couch in the living room, then she skipped back to the family room.

Noelle gave Aiden a hug. "Oh, I'm so glad you two came!"

"Me, too," Aiden said, then added, "Santa is coming tonight, *and* it's even snowing!" Captain had heard them come in, too, and was wagging his tail. Aiden gave the dog a big hug around the neck, then ran to join her nephews.

Then she gave Rachel a hug. "You look like you're feeling pretty good."

She smiled. "It's been a good day."

Noelle swallowed and couldn't put off asking any longer. "Is Jack not coming?"

Rachel gave a little shrug. "I think he's planning on it. He was still at work last I talked to him, so I told him a neighbor was heading this direction and could give us a ride. I'm sure he'll be here soon."

She nodded and walked with Rachel into the family room.

"Whoa! This place is magical," Rachel said as she looked around in wonder.

Noelle looked around, too, with fresh eyes. It really was. She was lucky to be able to spend her Christmases here.

Rachel looked at her and must've been able to sense her nervousness because she put a hand on her arm and said, "He'll come."

She nodded and went to help the others with the last-minute preparations in the kitchen. But by the time they all sat down to eat, Jack still hadn't come. She was starting to believe Rachel's and Hope's encouraging words a little less.

The sound of people chatting and the excitement of Christmas Eve filled the air as everyone passed around the plates of maple bacon Brussels sprouts, prime rib, mashed potatoes, stuffed mushrooms, and baked vegetables. But next to Noelle was an empty seat, and she felt that emptiness deep in her soul. Jack's absence made her realize exactly how much she longed to have him at her side and how much she enjoyed every minute of being around him.

Why wasn't he there? Did he decide he didn't want to be? Did something happen to make him not be there? Would he have told Rachel if he wasn't going to come, or was she just as clueless about the situation as Noelle was?

He had seemed that he wanted to accept Noelle's resignation and date her when she'd laid her heart out for him earlier today. She should've just waited for his answer then, instead of letting everything come down to tonight. Then she wouldn't be dealing with all this nervous anticipation right now.

"Happy birthday to Noelle," Porter shouted.

Everyone else replied with "And to Noelle, a good night!"

She grinned at everyone, even though she wasn't feeling it. Now that she'd experienced having Jack in her life, it no longer felt right to not have him there.

As they were all finishing up the meal, she saw Rachel, seated two chairs down from her, pull out her phone. She held her breath, hoping that it might be Jack and that Rachel would immediately turn to her with news.

But instead, Rachel just set her phone down and turned back to her conversation with Corbin, who sat on her other side. Noelle's shoulders slumped a bit as she exhaled and pulled out her own phone, checking to make sure that there weren't any messages that she hadn't felt come in. There weren't.

She turned to Aiden. "What do you hope Santa brings you for Christmas?"

"Paper," Aiden said while driving half of a Brussels sprout on the end of his fork around his mashed potatoes like it was a racetrack.

"Paper?"

"Yeah. I used all we had making snowflakes, and I want to make some more."

She chuckled. "You're a cool kid, Aiden."

Corbin stood up and put his napkin on the table. "I just realized that I forgot something we need for dessert. I'm going to go get it."

Everyone looked at him in confusion.

"It's Christmas Eve," her mom said. "You're not going to find a place that's open. What did you forget? I'm sure we can come up with something or do without."

He shook his head as he headed toward the front door. "No, it's important. We really need it." And then he rushed into the living room, and a moment later, they heard the front door open and close.

Noelle pushed some of her own food around her plate. She just wasn't feeling so hungry.

"Is everyone done?" Katie asked. "I'm super proud of this year's video, and I can't wait for you all to see it!"

Everyone carried their plates to the kitchen and cleaned them up, then went to the family room side of the room and piled on the couches and floor, leaning against the sofas and legs. As everyone snuggled into each other, Noelle felt the loss of Jack even more, even though she had a nephew on one side of her, a niece on the other, and two nephews on her lap. She would give anything to be able to snuggle into Jack right now.

The video started with a screen saying *An Allred Christmas*, then went to her mom, who was standing in the kitchen, with everyone working on their gingerbread train cars in the background. "One of my favorite things about Christmas is family. You are all a huge part of what makes this holiday so special."

Then her dad, obviously on the night of the Mystery Santa Hat activity, said, "I love you all. I want you to know that. I also want you to know that I still plan to take home the trophy tonight for Best Meal. That spot on our mantle has gone too long without a trophy, so we plan to give it all we've got."

A few of her siblings, siblings-in-law, nieces, and nephews told a few things about their favorite Christmas things or things they loved about this year, then it cut to Aiden. "And I heard Mom tell Mrs. Sowards that she was glad that Jack asked Noelle for help because Jack has been more smiley since he started hanging out with Noelle. And she thinks that he's pretty much in love with her. You know, the kind of love where there's kissing and marriage and sneaking food off each other's plates."

Everyone in the room laughed and commented and clapped at Aiden's clip, and Aiden beamed. Noelle's face flamed just as red now as it had when she'd heard Aiden say it during the hayride.

Then the video cut to Jack, and she sat up straight. "I didn't know you interviewed Jack!" It looked like it had been filmed the night of the hayride, too. She wasn't even sure how it had happened without her noticing. It was when they were at her parents' house, but she wasn't sure if it was before they had left or after they'd returned.

"It's hard for me to express how much I appreciate you all opening up your home and your traditions to Aiden and me and Rachel. This has all been unlike anything I've experienced. I grew up with all celebrations at Christmastime being non-existent. I thought I was fine without any of that because it was just the way things had always been. And I *was* fine.

"I didn't know how much I had needed things like this—family, traditions, acceptance—until you showed it to me and healed a part of my heart that I hadn't known had been broken."

Tears were falling down Noelle's face, and Weston turned from where he sat on her lap and said, "Are you sad?"

Someone passed a tissue down the couch to her, and she took it and dabbed at her eyes.

"I have loved seeing how much joy all of your traditions brought into Aiden's life as well. And I have loved seeing Rachel's face when Aiden tells her all about it. I know it has meant the world to her to know her son got to experience so many wonderful Christmas traditions. I will be forever grateful for you all."

The tears were streaming now, and she heard more than a few sniffles from everyone else. Now Tommy had turned in her lap to watch her with concern on his face, too.

The front door opened, and twenty heads all turned in unison to see who it was. "All right," Corbin said, "I got what we needed for dessert!"

And then he moved to the side, and Noelle saw Jack standing at the door, stomping the snow off his boots. He carried a couple of packages in one arm and a bouquet of beautiful red, green, and white flowers in the other, and she desperately wanted to be next to him.

As she extricated herself from her niece and nephews and the kids sitting on the floor who were using her legs for a backrest, Jack had made his way to where her mom had stood to welcome him. He handed her the flowers and said, "These are to say thank you for hosting tonight and for inviting us."

She thanked him and gave him a hug, then Corbin took the two packages from him and set them on a side table.

Then Noelle got free, stepped between what seemed like a dozen legs outstretched on the floor, and breathed, "You came" as she finally reached him.

He looked at her with the softest, sweetest eyes and said, "I wouldn't have missed it for anything. I got slowed down a little bit on the way here—a car slid through a traffic light and crashed into me."

Noelle gasped, grabbed hold of his arms, holding them out, and stepped back a bit, checking him over for damage.

He let out a soft chuckle. "I'm okay. The people in the other car are okay. The paramedics checked us all out and gave us the green light to head home. Our cars, not so much. But the people are okay." He smiled. "It looks like it's my car's turn in the shop while I drive a rental."

She wrapped her arms around him in a hug, so overcome with emotions that he was okay. And he was here. But then she heard the slightest *oof* of air escape him, and she pulled back. "Oh! You're injured."

"I'm okay. I'll probably be feeling it a bit in the morning, but I'm okay." He reached for her hand and tugged her a little closer.

She gazed into his eyes, trying to decipher what he was thinking, especially after hearing what he'd said during the hayride. "I saw your interview in Katie's video."

"Oh yeah?"

Noelle nodded.

"That was for your family. There's more I wanted to say to you."

She leaned in a bit closer like she was being pulled. "Like what?" Her words came out a little breathier than she'd intended, and his eyes shifted quickly to all the people she knew were behind her before they came back to her eyes.

She should probably offer to take him into the living room or something so they could have a private moment. But he was here, and he was safe, and he was looking at her with those amazing eyes of his, and she didn't think she could move her feet if she tried.

"Like how much I love that when you really smile, you get a dimple right there. Like now. And the way your eyes crinkle when you're amused. And when you bite your bottom lip ever so subtly when you're thinking or considering something new. And how you raise your left eyebrow slightly more than the right just before you share a brilliant idea.

"And the way you cock your head just slightly to the side when you hear someone talk about something that happened to them or when you notice someone is down, right before you jump in and do something to help. The way you look out for others. The way you put your all into everything you do.

"You are always so open with your emotions and your life, which has been both a blessing and a curse for me because it means that I've been falling in love with you every day for the past year and a half."

She blushed and looked down. Had he really noticed all those things about her? What had *she* been doing at work all this time? Except for the last few weeks, when she'd been hyper-observant of everything about Jack, she felt like she'd spent the year and a half before that being remarkably *un*observant and not nearly good enough for this man, despite all the kind words he said about her.

Then, like he could read her mind perfectly, he said, "I wasn't showing you the same courtesy you were showing me."

Her eyes flew up to meet his.

"I have kept myself professional and closed off at work because I think I should be." He took a deep breath. "A lot of people get an idea about who someone is and have a hard time seeing anything differently. Thank you for being willing to see beyond the only face I ever showed at work, even at times when I really didn't want you to see beyond that. In these past few weeks, it has felt like you could see straight to my heart."

His eyes were looking at her so earnestly, his voice slightly gruff, like the emotions behind what he was feeling were coming through. She felt all those emotions, too. "I haven't ever had anyone be that way with me. To see past the things that most people would see and be judgmental about, then not go any further.

"But you were never judgmental. You saw the real me, and, probably without even realizing what you were doing, you gave me permission to be the real me. I'm grateful for that because it has made me feel like I could open myself up to love. And I can tell you that I've never been as happy in my life as I am when I'm around you."

He gave her a smile that was sweet and soft and made happy fluttering in her chest.

"And I think I might be in love with you, too." He smiled that smile that she had seen so often over the past few weeks. The one she loved so much because it felt like it was only for her. "In fact, I'm sure of it."

She grabbed him by the front of his coat with both hands and pulled him in close. "You, mister, are one very amazing man, and I'm sure I'm in love with you, too." Then she pressed her lips against his. She wanted him to wrap his arms around her and maybe even lower her into a dip and kiss her like he had in the living room when they'd been decorating the tree.

But she knew that her entire family was currently right behind her, probably all leaning forward with rapt attention. So she pulled back quickly and grinned at him, a giddiness filling her to the brim.

Then she turned to face her family, which apparently gave them permission to stop watching in utter silence because a cheer went up from the entire crew, and they all stood and swarmed them in a giant, lopsided, very crowded group hug.

A few minutes later, they were all seated around the table. The seat next to her that had been empty at dinnertime was now filled with a man who had at one time seemed like a Grinch, yet now it was her own heart that felt like it had just grown three sizes.

Someone turned the lights out, and her mom carried a piece of caramel apple pie on a plate toward her, the candle in it glowing brightly in the darkness as everyone sang happy birthday to her.

At the end of the song, Sadie shouted out, "Be sure to make a wish!"

She smiled at Jack. "I did, and it already came true."

"Well, if that isn't a Christmas miracle," her dad said, "then I don't know what is."

Noelle chuckled, then blew out the candle.

CHAPTER EIGHTEEN

Jack

It hadn't mattered that Jack had spent twenty-seven Christmases not ever experiencing a Christmas Eve that he enjoyed. In a single night, tonight had made up for all of them. Aches from the car crash and all.

After the festivities had started to die down, Noelle had grabbed a thick blanket off the back of the couch and motioned for him to follow her out to the back patio. He'd picked up the present he'd brought for her and followed her into the snowy night, setting it on a small table. He would follow her anywhere.

They had been standing at the edge of the patio, blanket wrapping them both, for a good twenty minutes, watching the snow softly fall, their breaths making little puffs of clouds. The moonlight shone across the snow, giving everything an unearthly, magical glow.

She looked up at him from where she was snuggled in at his side. "I thought this Christmas would be terrible. Thank you for making it the best." Then she leaned her head against his chest, and he just wanted to stay like that forever. It didn't even matter that it was cold or that his back still hurt from the wreck.

"Oh!" She said, turning in the blanket he held around the two of them so that she was facing him. "You brought out a present for me!"

He chuckled and removed the blanket from around the two of them before placing it around her shoulders and walking to the small outdoor table shielded from the snow and picking up the package.

He leaned in close to her and whispered, "Happy birthday," before placing the package in her hands.

"Oh. It's heavy."

She set it back down on the table and started carefully opening the wrapping paper to reveal a plain brown box. She looked at him in question, then lifted the lid and gasped.

She pulled the snow globe out of the packaging and held it up to admire it. The globe itself was set in a red lantern-shaped housing. It had a small motor that constantly set the water inside in motion, and with its interior light, the swirling glitter looked as if the snow was falling like it was just beyond the roofed patio where they stood.

She didn't seem to have any words, so he stepped in close, pointing out the figurines in the globe—it was of the two of them, decorating their snow and stars Christmas tree during the Mystery Santa Hat activity. "I figured that since your gran-gran and you had made a snow globe-themed tree that snow globes were important to you. I found someone who custom makes these, and she was more than willing to do an extremely rushed order."

She brushed her fingertips along the curved glass. "Jack," she breathed, "this is incredible. It's our own little scene!"

He smiled at the look of wonder on her face, thrilled that she liked it as much as he hoped she would.

He placed a kiss on her temple. "And I hope we have many more in our future together."

She carefully set the globe back into its packaging, then turned and brought her chilly hands to his face, letting the blanket fall to the patio floor.

Her kiss earlier had been quick and sweet. When she kissed him this time, she seemed to pour everything into it. Her kisses were soft and tender. When he put his arms around her and pulled her in close, she wrapped her arms behind his neck, her kisses became something more. A thank you, a promise, an acceptance of everything that he was.

From somewhere around at the front of the house, they heard jingle bells ringing, and Noelle broke the kiss just enough to whisper against his lips. "That would be my dad."

A sound erupted from the family room, just beyond the closed patio doors, and, keeping their arms wrapped around each other, they turned to look. All the kids were running around, grabbing things, all the parents were standing up, and everyone started hugging each other.

"We should probably go back inside," Jack said, but not before placing one last kiss on her cheek, just in front of her ear.

As soon as they opened the door, Aiden came rushing up to Jack. "Santa is nearby! We need to get home and get to sleep because he's going to be coming really soon!" The excitement coming off of Aiden was palpable and contagious. Rachel was right—he was at the perfect age for Christmas. He was glad that Rachel had pushed Jack to help Aiden experience it all.

"Okay, buddy. Get your shoes and coat on, and make sure you've got all of your stuff."

Then he turned back to Noelle. "I don't want to leave." He leaned in close enough that his lips were brushing her ear and whispered, "But I've got to go be Santa."

"I don't want you to leave, either. But I am going to enjoy picturing you doing that tonight." Noelle gave him a smile that made his chest soar. "You go. We've got forever ahead of us."

He gave her one last smile and kiss. "We do."

EPILOGUE

Noelle

One Year Later

Noelle stood by all the coats piled high on the couch in her parents' living room, picking up one at a time and handing it to its owner as everyone said their goodbyes to each other.

"Happy birthday to Noelle..." Aiden shouted out.

And then everyone else joined in the chorus, "And to Noelle, a good night!"

She smiled, just like she always did whenever anyone did that on her birthday. Especially when it was Aiden. The kid she now got to call her nephew. That made her smile even bigger.

Once they all made it outside and she and Jack were splitting off to head to his car while Rachel and Aiden veered off toward theirs, Aiden turned and called out, "We'll race you back to our house!"

"No," Rachel said, "we will drive the speed limit or under on the way back to our house. We don't want Uncle Jack to get in a Christmas Eve car crash ever again."

"Right," Aiden said. "Don't speed, Uncle Jack. And don't wreck."

Jack chuckled, then saluted Aiden. "You've got it, buddy."

As they pulled away from her parents' house, Noelle said, "I wish we could've been in our new house by Christmas. It would be fun to have Rachel and Aiden sleeping over at our place this year."

That had been their original plan. But owners of the home in Mountain Springs that they were buying had a delay on the house they were building, so now they weren't going to be able to close on their home until mid-January.

Jack reached out and entwined his fingers in hers—something she would never tire of feeling. "It's okay. This Christmas already has enough firsts—we can save *First Christmas in our new house* for next year."

"True." And the house they were buying was so perfect for them and so beautiful, and so close to both of their families. It was worth waiting for.

"This year," Jack said, his eyes darting to hers for a quick moment before watching the road again, "is the first Christmas where I get to call you my wife."

"The first Christmas where I get to call you my husband. And the first Christmas where everyone on the hayride actually went to the church for our wedding instead of going caroling."

Noelle smiled at how perfect it had been. Her favorite activity led to her favorite day of her life.

Jack gave her hand a squeeze. "The first Christmas while you've been working at Anderton Advertising."

She had found the job quickly after she had quit working for Jack. And much to her surprise, she loved it. She thought she'd never find a place she loved as much as working for Jack, so it definitely eased the blow of not continuing to work for him.

"And the first Christmas where they put you in charge of planning the holiday party. And put you in charge of a million other things once they found out what a rockstar employee you are."

She chuckled. He always made her sound like she was more impressive than she was. Anderton's was a much bigger ad agency, so she often met with clients personally, which she still wasn't entirely used to. It made her wish he was there to introduce her to each new client because he always made her sound like she was capable of taking over the world. It gave her a boost of confidence every time.

"And," she said, dragging out the word, "this is the first Christmas where you had to be worried about the boss/employee relationship with Jess." Jess was the woman who had taken over her position after Noelle had quit a year ago today. As she was training her, she quickly became her best friend, so Jack hadn't quite gotten past having to navigate the waters of socializing with an employee outside of work hours.

"Yeah," he said dryly, "thanks for that."

She laughed heartily just hearing his tone. Then she gave his hand a squeeze. As they turned onto Rachel's street, she said, "It's our first Christmas seeing Rachel so healthy after being declared cancer-free."

Jack's smile seemed to fill his whole face.

"You really like that one, don't you?"

"I will never tire of seeing her so healthy. Ever." He pulled into her driveway just as Rachel pulled into her garage. "This is our first Christmas taking home the trophy for the best dinner."

"And I can't wait to put that trophy on our new mantle."

"Even though it's a trophy of the world's scariest-looking elf wearing an equally horrifying Christmas sweater?"

"Especially because it's of the world's scariest elf and horrifying sweater."

As they were both walking up to the front door, shivering in the cold, he said, "First Christmas where we know we'll be leaving the next day to go honeymoon in warm, sunny, not-at-all snowy Cancun."

Noelle moaned in anticipation. "I can't wait to soak up all that sun."

Before Jack opened the front door, he put an arm around her waist and said, "First Christmas where I get to say happy birthday to my wife." And then he planted a sweet kiss right on her lips.

Once they got inside, Aiden gave Jack his usual running starfish hug, then hugged Noelle, and they both pet Bailey as she nuzzled in between them all. They helped get Aiden to bed, read him the book *The Night Before Christmas*, then put out the presents when they knew he was asleep. After saying goodnight to Rachel, they got ready for bed and headed into the living room, where an air mattress was already blown up and waiting for them.

They shifted to get situated, bouncing each other on the air mattress with each tiny movement. Then, covers pulled up to her chin, Noelle lay her head on Jack's shoulder, snuggling into him. She turned her face toward his. "First Christmas where I get to wake up on Christmas morning right next to you."

He kissed her forehead and said, "Here's to many more firsts."

Want to read more Christmas romances by Meg Easton?

Get *Stockings, Snow, and Mistletoe*

Two full-length Christmas romances to snuggle up with and swoon over. Both are full of heart, humor, hope, and

all the magic of Christmas wrapped up in one holiday-filled collection.

Christmas at the End of Main Street:
All either of them wants for Christmas are some jingle bells, to deck the halls, and for everyone to stop finding them dates. This Christmas, Macie and Aaron are teaming up to make everyone believe they're dating each other so they'll quit trying to line them up with others. But as this fake relationship starts to feel real, can they overcome the obstacles in their way?

A *Kiss at Christmas*:
Kelli wants a perfect little Christmas. Parker just wants to ignore it. Both believe they're going to be spending the holidays alone. Until the owner of the company they both work for—a man who has a secret knack for matchmaking—invites a dozen employees to celebrate Christmas on the beach. Can they get past their workplace rivalry and take a chance that might just be imperfectly perfect?

Get COMING HOME TO THE TOP OF MAIN STREET free when you join Meg's VIP readers!

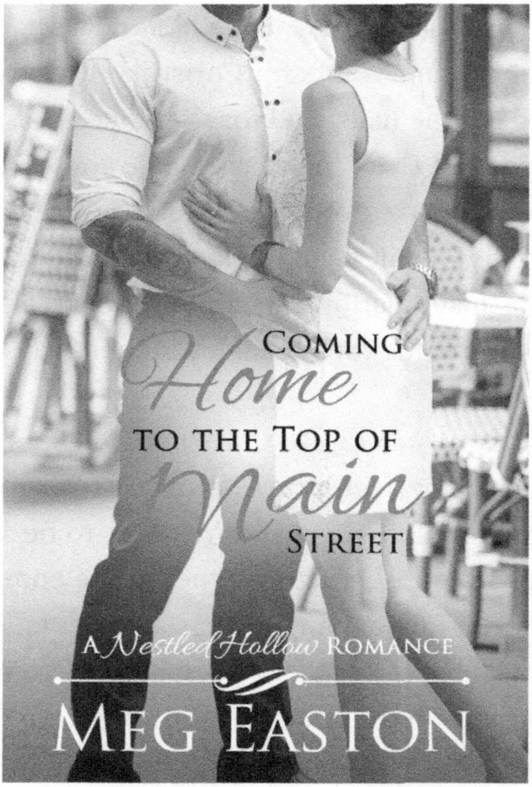

Tap here to join Meg's newsletter

OTHER BOOKS BY MEG EASTON

Nestled Hollow Romances

Second Chance on the Corner of Main Street

Christmas at the End of Main Street

More than Friends in the Middle of Main Street

Love Again at the Heart of Main Street

More than Enemies on the Bridge of Main Street

How to Not Fall romantic comedies

How to Not Fall for the Guy Next Door

How to Not Fall for the Wrong Guy

How to Not Fall for Your Best Friend

How to Not Fall for Your Ex

The Royal Palm Resort beach romances

A Kiss at Midsummer

A Kiss at Christmas

Silver Leaf Falls romances

Coming Home to Silver Leaf Falls

Love Started romances

It Started with a Sunset

It Started with a Note

ABOUT MEG EASTON

Meg Easton is the USA Today bestselling author of contemporary romances and romantic comedies with fun, memorable, swoon-worthy characters, and settings you'll want to pack up and move to. She lives at the foot of a mountain with her name on it (or at least one letter of her name) in Utah. She loves gardening, bike riding, swimming before the sun rises, and spending time with her husband and three kids.

You can find out more about Meg and her books at www.megeaston.com.

Made in the USA
Las Vegas, NV
30 September 2022

56306130R00121